Dear Jeffrey,

Well, I know you think I'm probably home, crying my eyes out, because you didn't go through with our wedding. But I've always known I deserve better than you—and I've finally decided to get it.

First, though, I've decided some changes are in order. So I say goodbye to the old Lorna Smith, with her no makeup and sensible shoes, the one who would never even talk to strangers. And hello to the new Lorna—with the wild hair *and* the desire to flirt with the first cute guy who comes along. And one has already. All right, Adam Gantry may be an uptight lawyer, but if anyone should know how to loosen him up, it's me!

Oh—if I think of it, I'll return the wedding gifts when I get back from my solo honeymoon in Palm Springs. *If* I get back...

Love, your *ex*-fiancée,

Lorna

Please address questions and book requests to: Silhouette Reader Service
U.S.: 3010 Walden Ave., P.O. Box 1325, Buffalo, NY 14269
Canadian: P.O. Box 609, Fort Erie, Ont. L2A 5X3

Runaway Brides

CHRISTINE RIMMER
TEMPORARY TEMPTRESS

𝒮𝒾𝓁𝒽𝑜𝓊𝑒𝓉𝓉𝑒 𝐵𝑜𝑜𝓀𝓈

Published by Silhouette Books

America's Publisher of Contemporary Romance

SILHOUETTE BOOKS
300 East 42nd St.,
New York, N.Y. 10017

ISBN 0-373-30140-5

TEMPORARY TEMPTRESS

A Letter from the Author

Dear Reader,

Oh, I do love make-overs. Always have. Just the whole idea of the nice/sensible/mousy girl getting her chance to be a little naughty and a whole lot glamorous is one of my very favorite fantasies.

Over the years I've written a number of make-over stories. But *Temporary Temptress* was my first, and thus holds a special place in my heart. To add to the fun, in this story the heroine gets her make-over in response to being left at the altar. To me, that seemed the perfect setup for a rollicking good read.

I just loved the heroine, Lorna. To be honest, I was going through a rough patch in my own life at the time. And I wouldn't have minded *being* Lorna. There she was at the beginning of the story, unceremoniously dumped by a guy who wanted more excitement in his life than he thought a mouse like Lorna could ever provide. So does she pine and whine and sulk? No way. Lorna goes on her Palm Springs honeymoon by herself! And there, with a little help from a special friend, she is transformed into the siren she's never dared to dream she could be.

Now, that's a real heroine. And for being so brave and gutsy, I gave Lorna the staid-but-devastatingly-sexy Adam Gantry for her hero. I hope you enjoy reading their story half as much as I enjoyed writing it.

All the best,

Christine Rimmer

Prologue

Adam Gantry shifted the car into park and switched off the engine and lights. He peered through the late-night darkness at the house he had sought and found by taking the address from Astrid's address file and consulting a map bought at an all-night liquor store.

The house was one of those low, flat-roofed structures, without any distinguishing features. Adam thought it a surprisingly average-looking place for an ex-lover of Astrid's to live in.

Wondering ruefully if he'd ever see a good night's sleep again, Adam rubbed the stiff muscles at the back of his neck. He had a problem with insomnia and hadn't been able to sleep last night. And tonight, of course, would end up a total loss. His eyes felt grainy, his tie too tight. He pinched the bridge of his nose between thumb and forefinger in a futile effort to massage away the tiredness, then loosened his tie.

Guilt, dread and anger had carried him this far. But now he hesitated. Was he doing the right thing? He spent several seconds debating, staring rather blankly at his watch. The time was 3:00 a.m. He really hated to disturb the house's occupants at this ungodly hour.

If he had any sense at all he'd give it up. Return to L.A. and get on with his life.

But he couldn't. He was too worried about Astrid. Growing up with her for a mother hadn't been his idea of the perfect upbringing. But still, she had done her best. He loved her, and he owed her. And the note she'd left behind for her stunned fiancé when she ran out on her own engagement party had rung a shrill warning in Adam's mind and heart.

Max,
My secret sister needs me in Palm Springs, so I must go to her at her hotel there.
     And I want to be honest with you, my darling. I must see Arthur Utulo before I can marry you. I was in love with him once, long ago. And he lives there now. I must have some time to be sure. Please understand.

                         Yours,
                         Astrid

Max had handed Adam the note without saying a word, and then told Adam very quietly that he wanted to be alone. Just thinking of the stunned, despairing expression on the older man's face made Adam's stomach twist with guilt.

Maxwell Hollander was the senior partner in Adam's law firm, Adam's mentor and the father he'd never had. Max never would have met Astrid Gantry if Adam hadn't introduced them two years before.

But worse than Adam's guilt, even worse than his fury at his mother for pulling such a cruel stunt, was his dread.

"My secret sister needs me..." she had written. What the hell was a *secret sister*? Adam was afraid he already knew. He was all too aware of his mother's fatal weakness for odd societies and fringe groups.

Adam was terrified that if he didn't get to her soon, she'd sign over everything she owned to this mysterious secret sister. He was afraid she was throwing away both her chance for happiness *and* her solvency. As her only child, he just couldn't sit by and let her ruin her life.

Positive that he was in the right, Adam left the car. He strode purposefully up the cement walk, past the crouching shadows of spiky-leaved century plants and a pair of runty yuccas. There was a wooden plaque beneath the porch light that read The Utulos.

Adam rang the doorbell. When there was no immediate answer, he waited a respectable ninety seconds and rang again. A light went on in a side window. He waited some more, and then the door, held by a chain, opened a crack.

A matronly middle-aged woman, her head covered by pink foam rollers and a flowered hair net, peeked around the door.

Adam's quick mind drew the logical conclusions. This had to be the ex-boyfriend's wife. The likelihood that he'd find Astrid wrapped in Arthur Utulo's arms had just greatly diminished.

"Yes?" Through bleary eyes, the woman peered at him warily. He knew that his clothes and manner spoke well for him, and he was careful not to present a threatening stance. He gave her a moment to look him over before he spoke.

"Excuse me, I'm sorry to bother you...." Adam began.

"It's very late," the woman murmured, looking a bit less wary.

"I know, but I'm trying to find someone and I was afraid if I waited until a more respectable hour, the—" he paused significantly, hoping he was taking the right tack on this "—trail would be cold."

The woman narrowed her squinting eyes even further. "Are you with the police?"

"No." He cleared his throat officiously, and then dropped his voice to a confidential whisper. "This is a private matter." He whipped out a picture of Astrid standing in front of Stellar Attractions, the hairdressing salon that Max's money had bought.

The woman gave the picture one quick look and then swore in a distinctly unmatronly manner. "I should have known."

"Then you've seen her?"

"What's she done?"

"I'm not at liberty to say. I hope you understand."

"I certainly do." She glanced over her shoulder, no doubt eager to get Astrid in as much hot water as possible before her husband could interrupt. "All I can tell you is, about seven tonight, she came into Icy Delights, the frozen-yogurt store that Artie and I own. She just strolled in bold as you please and pranced right up to the counter where Artie was ringing up a sale. 'Hello, Art,' she says in this low, sexy voice. Then she grabs him around the neck, kisses him right on the mouth in a way that left no doubt they'd once been, well, you know. Then she steps back, shakes her head, and prances on out. Artie swears he hasn't seen her in forty years, but I—"

"Enid, what the hell is going on out there!" The man's voice came from somewhere in the back of the house.

"Nothing, Artie!" She grinned at Adam, rather slyly. "He's sleeping in the back room tonight." She turned as footsteps approached behind her.

Then Artie, older than Enid and totally bald, was squinting around the door. "What's this? Man can't get no sleep in his own damn house."

"I'm sorry to bother you—"

"Then don't."

Adam stuck his foot in the door before Artie could slam it. "Please, Mr. Utulo. Just one question."

"Make it snappy."

"Do you happen to know where Astrid Gantry might have gone?"

Artie cackled. "Nope." He shook his head, and a gleam came into his watery eyes. "What a woman."

"Artie!" Enid screeched from behind him.

"She didn't happen to mention anything to you about a *secret sister*, did she?"

Artie shook his head. "Get your foot out of the door now, sonny. As you can hear, I got me a little domestic problem to take care of."

"Thanks." Adam removed his foot and Artie shut the door.

Adam stood on the cement walk for a moment, hearing the arguing voices behind the door and wondering what to do next. Then he returned to his car.

The problem was that he had no lead at all on this mysterious secret sister. A call to Rafael Potts, Astrid's assistant at her salon, had revealed only that Rafael "thought it was something to do with some women's group," which told Adam hardly anything. Calls to two or three of Astrid's closer friends had gotten him no more information. They all said they had no idea what he was talking about, but that Astrid always had been one to get involved with "interesting" people.

Intent on finding some kind of clue, no matter how minimal, Adam took the crumpled note from the glove compartment and, by the dim interior light, read it again.

My secret sister needs me in Palm Springs, so I must go to her at her hotel there....

Adam switched off the light and sat in the darkness, staring at the shadows of the surrounding mountains against the night sky.

How many hotels could there be in a resort town like Palm Springs?

"Too many," he answered his own question aloud with a weary sigh.

But what else did he have to go on? Zero.

He pictured Palm Canyon Drive in his mind. Several miles of main street, packed with exclusive shops, restaurants—and countless hotels.

Grimly, he slid the key in the ignition and started up the car again. If he intended to visit every hotel in Palm Springs in hopes that his mother had registered in one of them using her own name, he'd better get started. Somehow, he had to find Astrid before her "secret sister" took her for everything she was worth.

One

Lorna Smith was lazing abed in her honeymoon suite when a timid knock, barely audible in the bedroom, came at the sitting room door.

Lorna snuggled deeper beneath the satin sheets, feeling deliciously self-indulgent. Then she languidly rolled over. Her skin felt like silk, the result of a long, luxurious soak in a tub full of foaming bath salts. The bath salts had smelled like fresh strawberries and so had the special soap Astrid had bought for her to use.

Half-asleep, Lorna smiled, thinking of Astrid. Whatever else had gone wrong in Lorna's life, she'd certainly hooked the gold ring when she drew Astrid for her secret sister.

With her leather cosmetic kit under one arm, Astrid had driven all the way to Palm Springs to come to Lorna's aid. She had arrived at Lorna's hotel at eight the night before, wearing a man's tweed sport coat tossed rakishly across her shoulders and waving a bottle of expensive champagne.

"I'll have you know I stopped in the bar to get us this champagne," were the first words out of Astrid's mouth. Then the older woman had shivered. Trailing a cloud of musk, her signature scent, Astrid waltzed into the room, shedding the tweed jacket. "It was *freezing* in the bar. Why is it they always keep the temperature subzero in desert hotels?" She'd tossed her makeup kit on the sitting-room couch. "But, as luck would have it, I met the sweetest little redheaded man who loaned me his jacket. Chivalry, whatever they say, is far from dead. Now, call room service and order us up some champagne flutes and let's have a toast to sisterhood—and to your new freedom that you're going to thoroughly *enjoy*!"

Now, the morning after, Lorna indulged in a contented yawn. With her eyes still closed, she went on smiling. As Astrid had so wisely pointed out, life was all in how you looked at it. Lorna could think of herself as jilted at the altar—or as set miraculously free. When you saw it that way, the choice was a simple one to make.

Lorna sighed, happily. It was going to be a beautiful day, because *she* was going to make it that way. After a while, she would get up and take a long, hot shower. Then she'd pamper herself with a leisurely breakfast in the hotel's best restaurant—not the coffee shop today. Oh, no. She'd eat slowly and pleasurably on good china in elegant surroundings. And then she was going to hit every boutique in Palm Springs, buy herself a whole new wardrobe—and not one single item in it would be her usual beige.

Lorna Smith might in actuality be nothing more than an ordinary, practical lady who owned a bookstore in Westwood. But that didn't mean she couldn't start dressing in bright colors. "If you want to be different, you have to be willing to change," Astrid had said the night before. And Lorna intended to take her secret sister's advice completely to heart.

Out in the other room, the knock came again, slightly louder and more insistent.

"All right, I'm coming!" Lorna sat up among the acres of bed linens and reveled in a long, lazy stretch. Then she allowed herself to gaze on her own reflection in the wall of mirrors on the other side of the room.

Her plain brown hair now cascaded down around her bare shoulders. Astrid had trimmed it in layers, so the natural curl became apparent, and she had frosted the ends, so it glowed with bronze highlights. Her makeup, which looked so good last night that she hadn't wanted to wash it off, had a smudgy look now, but it didn't matter to Lorna. Beneath the smoked teal eyeshadow, her blue eyes shone back at her, full of mischief and promise. She looked golden and decadent, she decided, in her apricot silk teddy and absolutely nothing else.

The tapping on the door came again. Lorna tossed back the covers and entered the suite's huge bathroom. A fluffy terry-cloth robe, provided by the hotel, hung on a peg behind the door. She snared it and stuck her arms in the sleeves, belting it haphazardly as she went to answer the knock.

When she flung the door wide, the response of the man waiting on the other side was extremely gratifying. He gulped and stared.

Lorna granted him a dazzling smile. "Yes?"

He stuttered out a nervous explanation. "I, uh . . . last night I loaned my jacket to the lady in the room across the hall. But when I asked about her at the front desk just now, they said she'd checked out already. I wonder if you . . ." His voice trailed off as Lorna casually rebelted her robe. It was obvious that he found Lorna quite attractive. He seemed to be mesmerized by the bit of apricot silk that rebelting her robe had revealed.

"I'd trade my Mercedes to be like you," Lorna had moaned to Astrid the night before.

Astrid had gazed measuringly back at her for a moment, and then replied, "No, be yourself. Always." A mysterious smile had crossed her full mouth. "Besides, you're going to be surprised at what a knockout you are once I'm through with you."

As the redheaded man stared at her with his mouth open, Lorna felt naughty—and wonderful. Her new look was having its intended effect. The poor man's face flamed as red as his hair.

"There's a siren inside of every one of us," Astrid had told her the night before. "It's only a matter of bringing her out."

Of course, Lorna had no intention of indulging the siren within herself full-time, but it couldn't hurt to flirt just a little every now and then. She upped the wattage on her smile, feeling like a completely new and beautiful woman, like someone just a little wild on the brink of a grand adventure.

She heard Astrid's voice again in her mind. "So what if your fiancé jilted you? Let him go. Someone better will always come along—take it from a sister with a wealth of experience in games of the heart. Now. To go ahead with the honeymoon anyway was a stroke of genius. But you ruin the whole idea if you just sit here in your room and mope." Green eyes flashing, Astrid had waved her expensive shears, which glittered brightly in the light of a nearby ginger jar lamp. "What you need is adventure, something different and utterly wild. First, though, we get rid of the Marian Librarian hair and brighten up the makeup. We're talking makeover here, darlin'. We're going to totally change your self-image, starting with what you see when you look in the mirror...."

The redheaded man, still waiting for his coat, cleared his throat uncomfortably. Lorna went on smiling.

What a wonder Astrid was, Lorna thought with fondness. Astrid was the sister she wished she'd had, the mother she should have had, a true friend for life. Astrid was— She paused in her mental testimonial as the young man's first words to her suddenly sunk in. "Excuse me, I wasn't listening," Lorna said. "Did you say Astrid had already checked out?"

"That's what they told me at the desk."

Lorna frowned. She'd thought perhaps she and Astrid would hit the stores together today. For a moment she felt cheated. But then that sense of promise and excitement, Astrid's gift to her, overrode the rest.

Of course. How like Astrid to do what needed to be done and then be on her way. Like a modern fairy godmother, Astrid had waved her magic wand. And like a fairy godmother, she'd disappeared before the dawn. And, of course, they would meet again in L.A. soon enough.

Lorna's admirer made a questioning noise in his throat. Lorna realized she'd kept him standing there waiting for several minutes while she privately rhapsodized about Astrid.

"I'm sorry. Your jacket, you're looking for your jacket?"

He nodded, smiling bashfully, and she noticed a gap between his two front teeth. She thought it charming because it suited him, with his shyness and his ready blush.

"Yes, I think I can help you there." She asked him his name and he said, "Teddy." She stepped aside and gestured him into the suite.

The jacket was draped over one arm of the couch. She picked it up and gave it to him.

"Thanks," he said. He was looking at the champagne bottle, upended in the bucket of melted ice, at the two champagne flutes on the glass coffee table. "I hope I didn't disturb you."

Lorna grinned and took his arm to lead him back to the door. "Well, I *am* on my honeymoon."

"Oh, I'm sorry. I really am." He was blushing furiously. "I hope your husband—"

They had reached the door, which stood wide open. Lorna went on tiptoe and kissed him on the cheek. "Don't you worry about him," she said. "He's a very sound sleeper. In fact," she lowered her voice to a confidential whisper, "until you brought him up, I'd forgotten all about him."

Teddy blinked and his blush spread, until even his ears turned red. He looked nervously at the half-open door to the bedroom. "Er, ma'am..."

"Lorna," she said.

"I really have to go now."

Lorna shrugged, and tried to keep from giggling out loud.

"And ma'am..."

"Yes, Teddy?"

"You really shouldn't talk like that." He was already backing down the hall.

Lorna leaned against the doorjamb and crossed her arms beneath her breasts. "I just have no idea what's gotten into me."

Teddy, visions of a large and jealous husband presumably flashing through his brain, had reached the elevator. He barely pushed the button when the doors slid wide. He disappeared inside, not glancing in Lorna's direction again.

Remaining propped against the jamb, Lorna stuck both fists in the pockets of the robe, looked down at her bare feet, which had been so beautifully manicured by Astrid, and realized she'd probably carried the joke a bit too far. She'd liked Teddy. And teasing him about her nonexistent husband had been rather mean. In her own mind, of course, the joke had been on herself. But Teddy hadn't known that.

Mentally chastising herself, Lorna pushed a strand of bronze-tipped hair behind her ear and then captured her index finger lightly between her teeth. The new Lorna might be wild, she decided, but in the future she was going to stop short of being mean.

Softly, behind her, someone coughed. Lorna turned her head toward the sound.

A man stood, behind and across from her, in the open doorway to the suite that had been Astrid's. Over six feet tall and expensively dressed in a pin-striped suit over a white shirt, he wore cordovan shoes and a nubby silk tie of a deep maroon that was echoed in his precisely folded pocket handkerchief. Thick, dark blond hair was neatly trimmed around his squarish oval face. His jade-green eyes assessed her coolly.

Though he appeared a little tired, and his tie was slightly askew, everything about him shouted success—and the absolute assurance that things would always go the way he made them go. He was precisely the sort of man the old Lorna would have thought too exemplary to be true. She would have been intimidated by him. But the new, slightly naughty Lorna, decided he was smug and superior and not her type at all.

Having defined him as of absolutely no interest to her, she didn't have to be mortified that he had probably just observed her kissing a strange man goodbye in the hallway while wearing little more beneath her robe than a wisp of silk and the lingering scent of strawberry bath salts.

"Sorry to interrupt your thoughts," he said in a quiet, well-modulated voice. His hesitation before the word "thoughts," told her clearly that he'd already assumed her most strenuous mental activities revolved around such quandaries as what to do about a broken nail and how to get rid of one boyfriend before the next arrived.

Lorna decided she loathed him. If he wanted to think of her as wild and naughty, well, fine, let him think it. She lounged more obviously against the door. "Exactly how long have you been standing there?" Though she didn't care in the least what he thought, she couldn't help asking how much he'd seen.

"Long enough," he replied. Lorna felt the flush creeping up from between the fluffy facings of her robe and ordered it back down. At the end of the hall, the elevator doors slid open again. The man glanced toward the sound. There was something in the movement, in the way he tipped his head, that Lorna found obscurely familiar. The doors glided shut again, no one getting on or off. Green eyes focused on Lorna once more, and the moment of familiarity ended.

The interruption had served a useful purpose, though, in giving her time to realize that this standoff in the hall with an arrogant stranger was not one bit wiser than teasing the bashful Teddy had been. The new Lorna needed a lesson in discretion from the old. She reached for the door handle.

"Wait a minute, Ms.—?" He managed a reasonably polite smile. "I didn't catch your name."

"I didn't throw it," she snapped tartly, then relented enough to tell him. "Lorna Smith."

He gave her a disbelieving frown, as if to say, *Naturally, all women like you have the last name Smith.* Lorna set her shoulders and glared right back.

"Just one question, Ms. Smith," he went on after a moment.

"All right."

"The woman who was staying in this room—do you happen to know where she went?"

"What woman?" Lorna asked without missing a beat, feeling a strong protectiveness toward Astrid well up within her. She had no idea what this man wanted Astrid for; maybe Astrid didn't want him to find her. And besides, she also had no idea where Astrid had gone.

"Blond, sixty but looks younger." The man rattled off a shopping list of Astrid's physical attributes in a deep, businesslike voice. "Green eyes. About five foot seven. I have a picture." He reached into his inside jacket pocket.

"No," Lorna shook her head. "I'm terribly sorry, but I can't help you at all." She shut the door in his handsome, overbearing face.

Adam stared at the closed door and debated whether or not to knock. The woman knew something; he was sure of it. As a lawyer, he was trained to notice every nuance of voice and gesture for clues to the truth beneath an artful lie. He'd seen the flash of indecision cross that gorgeous face when he'd mentioned his mother. The little temptress was hiding something. Adam raised a determined fist and rapped sharply on the door.

"Go away," the infuriating creature on the other side called after a moment.

He knocked again.

"I'm going to call Security," she threatened in a sweet little singsong, still not opening up.

Adam waited. He was betting she wouldn't be able to resist checking to see if he'd truly gone. Beautiful, provocative women like this one were like cats—too curious for their own good.

But Ms. Lorna Smith did the unexpected. Minutes passed, and she didn't reappear. Since she was all he had that even remotely resembled a lead, he knew he was going to have to wait her out.

Disgusted and annoyed, he went back across the hall to the suite he'd rented when the desk clerk had told him Astrid was already gone. He took the small vanity chair from the dressing area and, with the door open just a crack, positioned himself to be ready when his quarry ventured out of her lair.

The time seemed to creep by. Adam spent it studying the pattern in the Navaho rug underfoot, staring at the prints on the walls, and listening to his stomach, which hadn't been fed since the afternoon before, complain.

Precisely forty-seven minutes later, his patience was rewarded. She emerged, humming and smiling to herself. All that wild chestnut-and-gold hair was piled every which way on her head, so that little strands of it corkscrewed down her neck as she turned to lock the door of her room. Surprisingly, she was wearing a perfectly modest pair of tan Bermuda shorts and a simple white shirt.

He considered following her surreptitiously, and then felt like a fool. This was hardly international intrigue, after all. He wanted an honest answer as to what she knew about Astrid, and nothing more. Therefore, sneaking around behind her while she cut a swath through the Desert Fashion Plaza would be a ridiculous exercise in overkill. If she knew anything about his mother, or the "secret sister" sect, Adam would find out soon enough—by demanding the truth.

In fact, watching this bronze-haired seductress, obviously fresh from an invigorating shower—he, of course, hadn't dared leave his post for a shower, though his fastidious nature cried out for one—and ready to while away her day prowling Palm Springs for new diversions, he began to feel more than a little provoked. And then it occurred to him that feeling provoked was irrational. He didn't even know this woman; what she did with her time was no business of his. Realizing he was responding irrationally provoked him even more.

Disgusted with himself, furious with Astrid and fed up with this woman whom he didn't even know, he quietly rose to his feet, stepped silently into the hall and inquired in a voice so level and controlled it would have sent the paralegals at Engalls, Hollander and Gantry running for cover, "Ready for breakfast?"

Lorna spun around.

So he hadn't left after all, she thought. It appeared he'd been lurking in Astrid's suite, waiting for the chance to pounce. He strode toward her, looking so calm and determined that she had to admire his composure, at least. She noted with a wayward stab of satisfaction, though, that his tie was even more askew than it had been when she'd shut her door in his face. Mr. Impeccable, as she'd begun secretly to think of him, was becoming more peccable by the moment.

"Not with you," she replied in dulcet tones.

But he'd already taken her arm. Surprised by the warmth of his touch, she fell in step with him.

"I thought I said no," she told him without much conviction as they waited for the elevator.

"A lady always has the right to change her mind," he countered pleasantly. His stress on the word lady was so faint that she wisely decided to let it pass.

Two

In the hotel's best restaurant, Georgia O'Keeffe prints of calla lilies and hibiscus flowers graced the walls. The colors were soothing ones of turquoise sky and golden sand.

Mr. Impeccable ordered eggs Benedict, tomato juice, buttermilk, an extra English muffin, a side of pancakes and cantaloupe. "I haven't eaten since yesterday," he explained somewhat defensively on observing her awed expression.

Lorna ordered coffee, melon and a poached egg.

"You should give up coffee," he remarked imperiously when the waiter had left them. "And it wouldn't hurt you to have toast. Grains are a mainstay of any balanced diet."

She stifled a groan. Not only impeccable, but an expert on nutrition. The old Lorna would have been licking his cordovan shoes. "I'm watching my weight."

"Why?" He drank from the glass of tomato juice that appeared at his elbow. "There's nothing wrong with your weight."

"My Lord. That was almost a compliment."

He lifted an eyebrow at her. "You're beautiful. You know it. I know it. It's reasonable to assume that all the men you know know it. Is it something you also need to have talked about all the time?"

The acid smile she tossed him would have eaten through lead. "I'm insecure." He snorted disbelievingly in reply.

A few minutes of weighted silence ensued, while Lorna wondered what had possessed her to ruin her morning by having breakfast with—"What is your name, anyway?"

"Adam Gantry."

Luckily, Lorna was not in the middle of a sip of coffee, because she surely would have choked on it.

Of course, she thought grimly, schooling her features to reveal none of her surprise. Mr. Impeccable was Astrid's son.

In her memory's clear vision, she could see Astrid, sitting cross-legged in a straight-back chair at the June Street library where they met every week.

"I love my son very much," Astrid had said. "And I'm proud of him. He's only thirty-six and already a partner in his corporate law firm. He works hard and he's extremely responsible. But he's, well, stuffy and bossy, and he's never approved of the way I live my life. His father died before he was born. In Korea, sad to say. And unfortunately, I hadn't gotten around to marrying the dear man before he stepped on a land mine and went to his reward. I don't think Adam's ever really forgiven me for making a baby without a ring on my finger. Adam's so proper and perfect, you see. He finds it extremely imperfect that I never provided him with a daddy.''

Across from her, Adam spoke with gruff accusation. "You know who I am."

Lorna made herself sigh airily. "Oh, do I?"

"Give me the truth, Ms. Smith. Who are you and what do you know about Astrid?"

Not until you're honest with me, Mr. Impeccable, she answered silently. She asked, all innocence, "Is your name supposed to mean something to me?"

"Does it?"

She pretended to consider, then answered, "Well, there is the fact that it's perfect."

"That's all?" he demanded. She merely smiled. After a moment's pause he went on suspiciously, "What do you mean, perfect?"

She started on the melon, quite pleased with herself to have regained her equilibrium so quickly after learning who he was. "It fits you, that's all. Adam. Number one and unflappable. Your last name's somewhat out of character, though. It's a little, well, dashing. But don't worry. Looking at you, I can see that you've utterly squashed any dashingness that might be lurking deep down inside."

"That takes a load off my mind," he muttered drily.

"I'm sure it does."

"Is there anything else you've discerned about me merely by learning my name?"

"Only that you have some sort of really distinguished and enviable profession, am I right? One at which you just naturally excel. I have it." She batted her eyes at him, provokingly. "A lawyer. Corporate law, probably."

He straightened his tie. "Admit it. You know who I am."

"I'm admitting nothing."

"You look uncomfortable."

"Do I? I'm not."

"Would you like me to change the subject? Stop pressing you for how you know what kind of work I do?"

"That would be lovely," she said. The waiter slid her poached egg in front of her. She poked her spoon at it.

"What shall we talk about instead?" he prodded.

Lorna shrugged and swallowed a bite of egg. "Why don't you tell me?"

"All right. Let's get back to Astrid."

Well, she thought, I walked right into that one. "Who?" she asked, feigning ignorance.

He precisely spread butter on his stack of pancakes. "Come on, Ms. Smith. I know you've at least talked to her. I saw it in your eyes when I first mentioned her to you. Even the type of woman you are can't hide the truth all the time."

"Have I just been insulted?" Lorna queried lightly.

"Not unless you find honesty insulting."

Lorna could almost have dumped her empty melon rind in his lap. Honesty, indeed. The man certainly had nerve, to sit across from her and talk about truth when he wasn't even admitting his own identity. Deciding self-righteously that her own deception was totally justified, she said in a sexy little purr, "Hmm. The *type* of woman I am...and just what type is that?"

He looked up from his meal, scanning her casually pinned hair and the smoky shadows above her eyes that Astrid had taught her to apply so artfully. His glance lingered on her full, lushly tinted lips. "Wild. Footloose. A woman who never worries about who'll pay the bill, because there's always some man falling all over himself to grab it."

She looked back at him levelly. "You can't be sure I'm like that."

"Can't I?"

"You don't know me at all."

"Yes, I do, Lorna Smith. I know you all too well." His quiet, polished voice was suddenly like velvet, his jade eyes shadowed.

In an arrested moment of crystal-clear perception, Lorna understood that this too perfect, arrogant man did indeed find her beautiful.

And bad.

And probably dangerous to know.

He was drawn to her, just as surely as the shy Teddy had been, because she represented the power and magic that all sirens promised, as well as the imminent risk of destruction at their hands.

Such a realization was intensely exciting. Her heart beat a little faster, and she felt a delicious surging in her blood. A hectic flush rose to her cheeks.

"Stop it," he ordered, as if she'd done something overtly sensual. He very carefully wiped his mouth with his napkin, and then slipped the soft linen beneath the lip of his plate.

As she had in the hallway when Teddy had disappeared in the elevator, Lorna felt chastened. What in the world was happening to her, anyway?

One part of her wanted to look straight into Adam's eyes and tell him the whole truth and nothing but the truth: that she was really just an ordinary, everyday kind of person. That she owned her own business and paid her own way. That she kept the figure he admired through watching her diet and exercising three times a week without fail. That she was going through a crisis due to being stood up at the altar. That therefore she needed to kick up her heels and behave a little recklessly to get over the natural reactions of hurt and insecurity.

It was the truth. You could never go wrong by telling the truth....

Adam was watching her guardedly, that shadow of suppressed desire in his eyes.

That shadow would disappear, of course, once he learned who the *real* Lorna Smith was. It shouldn't matter that it would; she was never going to see him again, anyway. Not to mention the fact that any desire he might be denying was for someone who didn't really even exist.

But then, if she did reveal her true self, how would she explain her overnight transformation without admitting that she *did* know Astrid, after all?

And then, coming right down to it, what in heaven's name was he after Astrid for, anyway? And if Astrid didn't want to see her son right now, what kind of a secret sister would Lorna be if she gave him any clues that might tell him where to find her?

"Just tell me what she said to you," he prompted, reading her silence, correctly, as a weakening in her stance.

Stalling, Lorna made an elaborate show of pulling her compact from her purse, applying lipstick and powdering her nose. "Why in the world are you after this poor woman, anyway?" she asked at last.

"Then you admit that you talked to her?"

"Did I say that?"

"Did she tell you anything about—"

Lorna cut him off, not wanting to hear more and be drawn in. "Slow down, Counselor. You're leading the witness."

He shifted in his chair, no doubt planning his next interrogatory attack. The light from a nearby window fell across his face, casting his strong features into sharp relief. He looked stern enough to be one of the faces on Mount Rushmore.

"Are you going to answer any of my questions?" he demanded when the silence had stretched to the breaking point.

Lorna considered this query, and then demanded more firmly than she had asked before, "If you want me to answer your questions, I have a right to know why you're chasing this woman."

"It's a private matter."

"That tells me nothing. Did she do something illegal?"

"Well . . ."

"Something illegal. Yes or no."

"Who sounds like a lawyer now?" he asked.

"You're stalling."

"All right. No, not precisely illegal."

"*Sort* of illegal?"

"No," he glared at her. "Not illegal, but unethical. She broke a promise to someone she loves. Now, will you let me ask a few of the questions?"

Lorna evaluated. Was what he'd grudgingly disclosed enough to make her betray Astrid? After all, she owed Astrid a lot for rushing to her side when her whole world seemed to have fallen apart and for showing her how to turn things around.

"No." Lorna reached for her purse. "No more questions." She pulled out her wallet.

"What do you think you're doing?"

Extracting several bills, she dropped them in the middle of the table. "Paying for my breakfast. Whatever you may think, no man pays my way."

"I didn't say—"

"You didn't have to say. You saw me kissing a man in the hall and you naturally assumed I make my living that way."

"I said you were wild. That doesn't mean I think you're a—"

"Please." She stopped him before he could say the ugly word. "There's no need to put too fine a point on it."

"Then pick up your money and sit down. I offered you breakfast, I'll pay for it."

"I'm finished eating, and I have things to do."

"Sit back down, we're not through here."

"Have a nice life, Adam Gantry."

Not looking back, Lorna wove her way between the linen-covered tables and through the reception area with its skylights and sun-speckled potted palms. Once out of the restaurant, she went straight to the bank of elevators in the main lobby.

She'd pushed the Down button for the parking levels when Adam caught up with her.

"That was childish and rude," he told her condescendingly.

She shoved the button again.

"Please be reasonable," he said.

"How many ways can I say it? I have nothing whatsoever to tell you, so our brief association is terminated."

"Lorna—"

The doors to one of the elevator cars opened, and Lorna found herself face-to-face with Teddy, who was wearing jogging shorts and shoes and a sweatband around his forehead, obviously fresh from the hotel gym. At the sight of Lorna, his blush seemed to start at his bare knees.

She decided to brazen it out. "Hi, there," she said cheerily. "Did you have a good workout?"

He gulped, and stared over her shoulder. Lorna realized that the bashful redhead assumed Adam Gantry was her big, jealous husband.

"Damn it, Lorna." Adam grasped her elbow. Lorna shook him off and stepped over the threshold as poor Teddy dwindled to the back of the car.

Persistent as a bloodhound on the scent, Adam followed. Before the doors closed, several others, including a blue-haired lady clutching a French poodle, and three teenaged girls laden with shopping bags, piled on behind them.

By the time her mind finally registered that the car was going up, Lorna found herself wedged between the back wall and the lady with the poodle, flanked by the furiously blushing Teddy on one side and the relentless Adam on the other. The teenaged girls giggled among themselves. The poodle sniffed disdainfully.

At the third floor, the teenaged girls got off, but two couples took their places. The lady with the poodle backed up until she'd squeezed herself between Teddy and Lorna. This left Lorna closer than ever to Adam, who obligingly moved into the corner and pulled Lorna back with him.

"Hands off," Lorna whispered.

They were fitted together like spoons in a drawer, Adam's large and warm hands resting firmly at her waist.

"Stop squirming," he ordered quietly. "Things are tight enough in here as it is." Lorna subsided as the car began its upward journey again.

In the seconds before they stopped at the next floor, she became all too intimately aware of him, pressed so close against her. The matte fabric of his slacks tickled the tender skin behind her knees, and his chest was hard and firm at her back.

Lorna stared miserably at the wet nose of the poodle, who seemed by now to radiate canine disapproval.

"What's the matter?" Adam's breath teased her ear, and she actually thought she detected a note of humor in his soft whisper. "Are you afraid he'll be hurt that you've found someone else so soon?"

"Who?" She tried to sound utterly guileless.

"The one with the knobby knees and the red face to match his hair." He kept his voice low enough that only she could hear.

The elevator stopped. One of the couples got off. Teddy saw his chance, and slid around the blue-haired lady and out just before the doors closed.

"Another day, another broken heart," Adam murmured, and rather sanctimoniously, too, Lorna thought.

"You really don't need to hold me so tightly anymore," she shot back sweetly. "There's plenty of room now... unless you're *enjoying* it."

His hands immediately dropped to his sides. She shifted a little closer to the scornful poodle.

The digital display above the door went right past her floor. "By the way, where are we going, anyway?" Adam asked with exaggerated nonchalance.

"I don't know about you. I'm going to my car."

"Where is it? On the roof?"

"No, actually." The car stopped at the top floor. The doors slid open. "I got on this car because I was trying to get away from you." She granted him a sugary smile.

"Didn't do you much good, did it, honey?" the blue-haired lady tossed over her shoulder as she and her poodle finally got off.

The ride back down to the parking level seemed to take longer than going up had, but both Lorna and Adam kept their mouths shut.

When the elevator finally discharged them, Lorna turned to him and arranged her face into its most stubborn lines. "Are you planning to follow me around all day?"

One corner of his mouth curled in a half grin. "Just until you tell me what I want to know. Unfortunately for both of us, you're the only lead I happen to have." The charm and humor in his face at that moment took her by surprise.

She dropped her obstinate stance, unable to maintain it while she was thinking how very attractive he was. She turned and marched resolutely toward her car.

Adam's steps fell in behind hers—and halted at almost the same time. "I'll be damned," he said quietly.

Lorna felt a sick dropping in the pit of her stomach, as she wished fervently that her eyes were deceiving her.

But they weren't, and in her heart she knew it. There, where her beautiful new Mercedes should have been, sat Astrid's car, a decade-old pink Cadillac.

Three

There was an envelope on the dashboard. Scrawled across it were the words *Lorna, the key's in your purse.*

"So you never in your life heard of anyone named Astrid," Adam accused from behind her.

Lorna opened her purse and felt for her ring of keys. "I never said that. Not specifically anyway."

"Where is she?"

"I have no idea. But she's taken my car, and if you don't mind, I'd like to find out what's in that envelope." She withdrew her key ring. Two strange keys were on it; her own car keys were not. Sometime during the evening before, Astrid had managed the switch.

Adam waited, not interfering, as Lorna unlocked the car door, reached in and took the envelope from the dashboard and slit it open. The paper was hotel stationery, but it smelled faintly of Astrid's perfume.

Lorna,
Remember you did say you'd trade your Mercedes, even if you weren't entirely serious.

The truth is, darling, that a little makeup and a haircut is not enough to accomplish your total transformation. You need ADVENTURE, as I mentioned last night. I'm going to see that you get it.

Your adventure should be an open-ended kind of thing—one you invent as it's happening. I think trying to get your beautiful car back will at least get you going in the right direction. But the whole point is that you remain open to whatever comes along.

Also, I have a few things to straighten out in my own life, and I need a dependable car to do it. Yours will fill the bill just fine.

The Caddy's been overheating lately, but it should get you as far as Prescott, Arizona, where I need to see an old flame. Pay a visit to Bucky O'Neill at ten tonight, and I'll be in touch with you there.

Yours,
Astrid

Very carefully, Lorna folded the scented paper and placed it back in its envelope. She put the envelope in her purse.

"Well?" Adam asked.

Lorna said nothing.

"Is it a valuable car?" Adam prompted grimly.

"My pride and joy. A Mercedes 450 SL."

His mouth formed a bleak line. "New?"

She nodded.

"I suppose you'll want to call the police."

Lorna considered.

"Lorna, are you all right?"

"Yes, fine," she mumbled distractedly. She leaned against the old Cadillac, and looked at the cement floor, folding her arms beneath her breasts.

In a puddle that had dribbled out from under the car, she could see the bright reflection of her carelessly pinned hair, like spun bronze in the halogen lights from above. Her face itself, though, was in shadow. In shadow like the real me, Lorna thought, and like Astrid's true intentions.

In a strange way, it all came down to belief. Did she *believe* in Astrid?

If she believed in Astrid, Lorna would need to forget about the car for the time being—as well as the substantial financial investment it represented. Lorna would need to have faith that her car, as well as her own immediate future, was in trustworthy hands.

On the other hand, if she didn't believe, then there was a flaky sixty-year-old woman out there somewhere driving her Mercedes.

Twenty-four hours earlier, there would have been no decision to make. The old Lorna would have raced to a phone booth and dialed the authorities.

"You know what?" she asked, half to her shadowed reflection and half to the man beside her.

"What?"

"It was beige."

Adam put his hands on her shoulders and turned her around until he could look into her eyes. "Lorna, I know you're upset. If you're telling the truth, you've just lost a very valuable piece of machinery. But I hope you'll try to understand. I have reason to suspect that Astrid is being manipulated by a fringe group of dissatisfied women who don't have her best interests at heart."

Lorna hardly heard what Adam was saying. She felt her lower lip quivering, and it wasn't with tears. "Adam. You poor man. You don't understand at all, do you? My car. It was *beige*." She tossed back her head and let the laughter ring toward the steel-and-concrete ceiling overhead.

A marvelous sense of excitement and anticipation swept through her. If she was deluded, so be it. She was going to follow Astrid's lure. It was going to be wild.

"Listen to me." Adam gave her shoulders a gentle shake. "Do you want to call the police?"

Her decision made, she became aware of Adam once more. His golden eyebrows were drawn together in a grim, resigned expression.

Lorna felt sympathy for him. He was worried about Astrid. Suddenly, Lorna wanted the deceptions cleared up—both his and hers. But she didn't quite know how to start, so she asked noncommittally, "Wouldn't you call the police, if you were in my position?"

He dropped his arms from her shoulders and glanced away. "I imagine so."

"But you don't want me to do it, do you?"

"Stealing a car is grand theft," he muttered, perhaps more to himself than to Lorna. "She'll have to deal with the consequences, that's all."

She touched his sleeve. "Adam?"

He turned, and in the tilt of his head, the green eyes with a sadness in their depths, she saw Astrid. And she couldn't let him worry anymore. "I'm not calling the police. Astrid and I traded cars, that's all."

He looked grimmer than ever, standing there so stiffly in his expensive suit. "You're sure?"

"Of course."

His expression left grimness behind and became completely impassive. "That's not what you said a few minutes ago."

"I was surprised, that's all. Trading cars was sort of an, er, open-ended kind of thing. I mean, it was something we talked about, but never really firmed up. You know?" Lorna cringed inwardly at how forced her explanation sounded. If she were listening, she wouldn't believe herself for a moment.

Apparently, neither did Adam. "Who are you, and more importantly, *what* are you to my mother?" The voice was one of steely command.

Lorna decided she could no longer afford to take a defensive position in this conversation; she was just too culpable. But Adam Gantry had a few things to answer for, too. "Oh, so now you're ready to admit that Astrid's your mother?"

"Since you obviously knew it all along," he countered without a pause, "why didn't you say so?"

"I was waiting to see what you were up to. I care about Astrid. And I want to respect her wishes. It's logical to assume that if she hasn't let you know where she is, it's because she doesn't want to see you right now."

Her argument was reasonable. Adam wisely decided to go back to his other point. "Who are you, Lorna Smith? And how do you know my mother?"

A station wagon pulled in a few spaces over. A harried-looking young couple and three rambunctious children climbed out of it. Lorna waited until the parents had herded the kids to the elevator before giving him an answer to the second half of his question.

"We're in a support group together. She's my secret sister."

"I should have known," he said softly.

"We're committed to *being there* for each other in difficult times. It's a way of extending and intensifying the benefits of our weekly meetings, to have one other woman you can count on no matter what."

"And, in this situation, who's *being there* for whom?"

She scrunched up her nose at his sarcasm, but did her best to make her reply reasonable. "Astrid came to Palm Springs to help me out of a...negative frame of mind." Inwardly, Lorna shook a finger at herself. She knew she should make a clean breast of it, tell him the plain truth: she'd been jilted and she was nursing a broken heart. But it just wouldn't come out.

Adam Gantry had no idea who she really was: plain, practical Lorna, an unremarkable woman with about as much sex appeal as a profit-and-loss statement.

"You're a wonderful woman, Lorna," her fiancé had told her. "But I've fallen in love with someone else. I just can't see myself spending the rest of my life with a woman whose spice rack is always in alphabetical order. You're perfect, and I just couldn't live with that day after day."

Adam Gantry, on the other hand, didn't think she was perfect. Far from it. To him, she was exciting—a forbidden siren who tempted every man in sight. It was wonderful to be the seductress in a man's eyes for a change, even at the cost of complete honesty.

But lying was wrong. She shouldn't go on doing it.

As Lorna waffled, Adam continued his attack. "Where is Astrid now?"

"I don't know, Adam. She came to my room last night, and she was gone when I woke up this morning."

"Gone where?"

"She didn't say." It was another half truth, since the note in her purse told more. But Lorna couldn't show Adam the note, because that might be betraying Astrid's trust.

"Let me see that letter," he said, as if he'd read her thoughts.

Lorna shook her head. "The letter was meant for me, not you."

He held out his hand. "The letter," he reiterated. "Now." He took a step toward her, no doubt trying to intimidate her with his masculine size and presence.

Irritation replaced indecision, as she backed toward the acres of chrome on the grille of the Cadillac. Adam Gantry had no right to demand to read her mail. "I can just see you in the courtroom," she taunted, "turning every hostile witness in sight to a mass of quivering jelly."

He made a grab for her purse, she whipped it behind her back. "Damn it, Lorna..."

With elaborate provocativeness, she leaned toward him and walked her fingers up his shirt front. "Tell me why you're following her." She gave a tug to his tie.

He wrapped his fingers around hers. The touch was electric. That smoky, hungry look moved in his eyes again as it had during breakfast. The fascination of the new Lorna was working its magic. It took an effort of will, she could see, for him to hold to the subject. But he managed.

"What is this *support* group?"

His hand was warm over hers, sending tingling sensations down her raised arm. "Nothing mysterious," she said. "A group of women. We meet once a week. We share our feelings, our hopes and disappointments, what goes right and what goes wrong in our lives. We listen and talk and try to help each other." Her voice, she realized vaguely, was like the purring of a petted cat.

"That's all?" The prodding question held an unmistakably husky undertone.

There was a war going on inside him, Lorna observed. His mind didn't trust her, but the rest of him was captivated by her allure. His little finger moved, slightly, a feather-light caress against the skin of her wrist. Lorna, mesmerized by how wonderful it felt just to have his little finger doing that, drew a breath deep into her lungs and licked her lower lip.

"Yes, Adam. That's all."

His grip became infinitesimally tighter. "It would be nice if I could believe a word you say."

Lorna's whole body seemed to be warm and shivery-cold at the same time. The sensation centered in the hand Adam grasped, and was sent out and down through her body by the tiny action of his stroking little finger. Jeffrey, her two-timing fiancé, had certainly never made her feel this way. She was having trouble thinking about anything but how to *keep* Adam making her feel this way.

"Whether you believe me or not, I have Astrid's wishes to consider," she told him, still sounding like a well-stroked cat. "She'll find you when she wants to see you."

"By then we both know it could be too late." Could eyes devour? Adam looked at her as if his could do just that.

"Too late for what?" Lord, Lorna decided, she really did want to be devoured. Right now. In this parking lot. No matter how many families in station wagons drove up. It was naughty and it was irresponsible, but she wasn't herself. Not her *old* self, anyway.

"I think you know what," he said. And then he was suddenly speaking aloud what they were both thinking. "You'd better tell me not to kiss you. You'd better do it now."

She smiled, and she knew the smile was full of forbidden promises. "I think you should kiss me first. Then I'll make up my mind whether I should have let you or not."

"You're so bad," he said, and there was humor in his voice, along with the roughness of desire. "I've spent my whole life avoiding women like you. Women like my mother. You never think of the consequences of your actions."

"Um. Yes. Very smart, to avoid women like me." She lifted her mouth in brazen invitation. "After you kiss me, you can start avoiding me again. I promise."

His lips hovered a fraction above hers. "Women like you never keep their promises."

"Maybe I'm different than other women like me."

"Tell me another one."

"I *always* keep my promises."

"Liar."

"But it's the truth...."

"Shut up." The command was infinitely tender.

"Really, Adam. I'm telling the—"

Her protests were cut off, since at that moment Adam Gantry's self-control lost the battle with his senses. His lips touched hers. Lorna sighed in delight. Adam released her hand and clasped her waist, bringing her closer. He nudged her lower lip, and she opened her mouth just a little. His tongue traced the inner surface of her lips, in a warm caress.

Lorna smiled against the kiss. Her arms found their way up his firm, broad chest until they encircled his neck, letting her purse dangle behind him by its leather strap.

"I wasn't going to do this," he breathed against her mouth.

"Oh, I know," she murmured back. "But I'm so glad you did."

He made a low, hungry noise then, and his lips went from teasing exploration to command as they closed over hers. His tongue slid inside, tasting deeper secrets, and she pressed herself against him, feeling marvelously beautiful and desired. She let her tousled head fall back. He cupped it with his hand, holding her in place so he could kiss her some more.

Then she lost his mouth, and a small sigh escaped her. But he was only laying a warm trail of tiny kisses down her neck to the collar of her white shirt, and then back up again. Then his lips were on hers once more, slanting the other way, staking once again their erotic claim.

Lorna heard the sound of leather soles on pavement and the drone of oncoming voices at the same time as Adam did. Three men in business suits were approaching. Lazily, Lorna opened her eyes enough to watch Adam lift his head at the intrusion. His stern face was somewhat flushed, but a gleam of challenge sparked in his heavy-lidded eyes. The men very scrupulously pretended not to see what he and Lorna were doing. He gathered Lorna closer against his chest.

As the footsteps of the men receded, Lorna realized the thrill of the moment had passed with the interruption. The beautiful, erotic kiss was over. And she was left with the warmth of strong arms around her and the most inappropriate wish that those arms would never let her go.

Just as she was wishing he might hold her forever, he released her. He put his hands on her waist and pushed her away, frowning slightly at the way she clutched her bag to her side, protecting it from any more sudden grabs he might attempt.

She studied his face, which was still slightly flushed. She decided he looked tired, beneath the flush and the powerful aura of self-control he possessed. She wanted to reach out, stroke his face, tell him—

Lorna stopped herself in midthought. She had nothing to tell him, she reminded herself firmly. She hardly knew him. And what he knew of her was a lie from start to finish.

Not a lie, she told herself a bit defensively. Not a lie, a fantasy. And there's nothing wrong with a little fantasy now and then. Nothing wrong at all.

"Give me the letter," he said.

Lorna took a fortifying breath and met his eyes. "Tell me why you're chasing her."

"All right," he muttered, "though I'm sure you already know. But I'll go through it step by step, and then you'll let me read that note."

"Correction. Then I'll decide whether to let you read the note."

Adam turned and leaned against the driver's door of the Cadillac, though he was clearly not the kind of man who ordinarily leaned on things. "She ran out on the best man she's ever known. His name's Maxwell Hollander and he's the senior partner of my law firm. They've been happy and they're totally in love, so it makes no sense at all. Max has locked himself in his room and won't see anybody, and none of Astrid's friends have a clue as to where she's gone. She left a note that her *secret sister* needed her and that she had to see an old boyfriend before she could marry Max."

"You found me through the note?"

He nodded. "It said you were in a hotel in Palm Springs."

"Whew." Lorna shook her head. "You went from—"

"—hotel to hotel until I found the one she was registered in. I ran into you, and I was sure you knew something and that's all. I was right."

"What about the old boyfriend?" Lorna wondered, thinking of the note in her purse. Astrid had mentioned a boyfriend in Prescott, too.

"I arrived here about 3:00 a.m.," Adam said, "and I found the boyfriend first. He was just as much in the dark about the whole thing as I am. His wife's story, though, was that Astrid appeared at their frozen yogurt franchise early yesterday evening, kissed him on the mouth in front of several customers and left."

Lorna considered this tidbit of information. "*Kissed* him. But why?"

Adam's shrug spoke volumes. "That's what I'm trying to find out. Now give me that letter."

Lorna hoisted herself up on the Cadillac's hood and crossed her legs at the knees like a teenager without a care in the world. Adam watched her with evident disapproval. She was positive the women he dated never sat on the hoods of cars. "Is this Max person threatening to sue her for breach of promise or something?"

"Of course not." Adam's voice was curt. "Right now, Max is too broken up to think of getting even. And that's not his style anyway."

Lorna put her hands behind her on the hood and leaned on them. "Then let Max chase her down." She recrossed her legs and added with finality, "Astrid deserves to be in charge of her own life and affairs, Adam."

She could tell by the rocklike hardness of his jaw that he was losing patience. "She's my mother. I introduced them. And she owns a successful hairdressing salon that was started with Maxwell's money." He impaled her on a lowering glare. "She's not going to lose that salon, Lorna. It's her future, and her security."

Puzzled by the determination in his voice, she said, "I don't see what you're so concerned about. If the business is thriving, I'm sure it can run itself for a while."

Adam spoke with iron firmness, each word clear and cold. "Understand me. I'm not allowing her to lose everything this time. No matter what tricks you and your *support group* have up your collective sleeves."

"What in the world are you talking about?"

"You're very good at playing the innocent. Too bad you haven't done or said one thing so far that I can trust, or I just might be tempted to believe you."

"Adam. Just explain what you're talking about, okay?"

"Weird groups," he said coldly. "Like yours. Like the hundred other causes and cults my mother's been involved in. Like the ashram in Oregon where they made her go barefoot in January and she ended up with no savings account and chronic bronchitis. Like the Save-The-Bluenecked-Grackle association in Santa Monica to which she donated five thousand dollars before learning there is no such thing as a blue-necked grackle to save in the first place. Or the crystal channelers in Vermont who charged her five figures for a bunch of rocks and an instruction sheet on how to connect up to her inner forces. Or the greasy-haired gigolo she invited to stay in her house because he swore he'd been her father in their last life. When he disappeared, it was with her collection of Lladro figurines and her compact disc player. The list is endless. Do I have to go on?''

Lorna sighed, thinking how tired he looked. ''No, I guess not. And I'm sorry that Astrid's been used, Adam. But it hasn't really damaged her. You have to see that. She's the most alive person I've ever met. And she's not bitter at all. So I'd have to say that, whatever she's done or is doing, it's probably the right thing for her. And she should be let alone to do it.''

Adam took her hand and very deliberately pulled her off the hood of the car. ''That's easy for you to say, especially if you're the next in line to take her for all she's worth.''

Lorna gaped up at him. ''You think I'm after your mother's money.''

His eyes were hard as emeralds. ''You. Or that strange group you belong to. Or maybe you just don't want her to marry Max, to be happy. There are a lot of dissatisfied people in the world today who'll go out of their way to see that others don't find what really counts.''

"Let me get this straight." Lorna spoke as slowly and deliberately as Adam had. "You believe I'm a member of an anticommitment fringe group out to break up your mother's engagement and steal her hairdressing salon?"

"Naturally it sounds ridiculous when you put it that way. Now give me that letter." His hand shot out and closed on her purse.

She whipped it out of his grasp. "No."

"I could wring your neck." Adam spoke through clenched teeth. "I'd get off with a reprimand, once the judge heard the circumstances."

"If Astrid wanted to see you—" Lorna clutched her purse and restated her position "—she would have told you where she was going. It's clear to me that she needs to be left alone right now."

"I have been inordinately patient, Lorna," he said in that so calm voice that Lorna was beginning to re-alize meant he was seething with tightly leashed fury. "I've let you tease and flirt and bat your eyelashes all through breakfast. I've played Sardines in the eleva-tor, going up and going down. I've stood in this park-ing garage for—" he glanced at his gold watch "—twenty minutes while you broke down because your car was stolen and then decided it wasn't stolen and then seduced me into making a display of myself kissing you—"

"Just a minute there." She glared at him. "You weren't fighting it too hard, and we both know it."

"I'm not finished. And then, after you proved I couldn't resist you, you demanded to know why I was following my own mother as a condition of telling me where she was going. Well, I kept my end of the bargain. You know why I'm after her. Now tell me where she's gone."

"I can't. It wouldn't be right. She's—" Lorna sought the right words "—very special to me. And when she wants to see you, she'll contact you herself, I'm sure." She hooked her bag over her shoulder and brazenly stepped toward him. "I have to go now. Please get out of the way so I can open the door."

"Give me the letter."

"Get out of my way." She reached for the door handle.

He calmly leaned against it, so she was forced to pull back her hand. "I intensely dislike what you're forcing me to do," he said.

"Please step aside." She did her best to look formidable.

For a moment they just watched each other, sizing each other up, like all adversaries have done since the dawn of time. And then Adam moved.

With a lightning swiftness that made Lorna gasp, he grabbed for her purse. And he got it, too. Lorna felt the strap slipping down her arm. In a split second, he would have it free.

With clutching fingers, she caught the strap before it escaped her completely. And, digging in her heels, she yanked—and fell backward, when the strap snapped in two.

"Ooof!" She landed on her backside in the puddle of dirty water from the Cadillac's damaged radiator. "You overbearing—" she sought a suitably crushing adjective "—stuffed shirt. Give me back my purse!"

"As soon as I see what she wrote," he replied. He'd already slipped the clasp and retrieved the envelope.

Lorna knew she had to think fast. "That purse is my property!" She pretended to try scrambling upright, and then let out a strangled cry. She clutched at her lower back. "Oh! Oh, no..."

Adam, who had just smoothed the note open, paused to look at her.

She went on clutching her back and contorting her face into a grimace of pain. She groaned tightly, convincingly.

He set her purse on the roof of the car and knelt down next to her, wary but concerned. "Where does it hurt?" His voice was careful, but gentle, too. She could see that he was the kind of man who would watch over the victim at the sight of an accident, whether he had anything to do with the situation or not. Lorna felt like the sneaky troublemaker he believed her to be and almost dropped her ruse of injury and let him read the note. But then she thought of Astrid, to whom her first allegiance was sworn.

"I... don't know. I tried to get up and..."

"Don't move. You might just make it worse." He put a soothing hand on her shoulder. It was the hand holding the note.

She gazed up at him, right into his eyes. "Oh, Adam. I'm scared."

"Don't be. I'm sure you just twisted something. In a minute, the spasm will pass and you'll be fine."

"You really think so?"

"Certainly."

"Oh, Adam." She touched his face, as if doing so could reassure her in her fear and pain. He blinked, and just as he did that, she moved her hand the fraction necessary to whip the note from his grasp.

He gazed at her in a kind of numb disbelief for a moment, just the time she needed to stick the wad of paper in her mouth and reduce it to a soggy mass.

His light brows drew together, like the clouds before a storm. "You little witch."

She chewed diligently, watching his face as he considered forcing her jaws apart and extracting what was left of his mother's note. He apparently decided against such a useless maneuver, since he did no such thing.

She swallowed.

He stood up. "I'd offer you my hand, but I'm sure you never needed it anyway."

With no difficulty, but some regret at having had to deceive him once again, she scrambled upright herself. "Adam, I had to do it."

Coldly, he took her purse from the roof of the car and held it out to her. "Tell me where Astrid has gone."

"I can't."

"You think you're going to just drive out of here in her car?"

"That's exactly what I'm going to do."

"I could have you picked up. I could say you stole it."

"Come on, Adam. Then I'd just say we traded cars. When they found Astrid, they'd learn I was telling the truth."

"Maybe, but you'd have to tell them where to find her, wouldn't you?"

She gazed at him levelly. "No. I wouldn't tell them a thing. I'd say just what I'm saying to you. That I don't know where she went and she'll turn up when she's ready. You see, I'm on a kind of open-ended vacation, Adam. And if I have to spend it in a Palm Springs jail, well, that's just how it's meant to be as far as I'm concerned."

He shook his head, and there was a musing expression on his stern, handsome face. "This isn't the end of it, Lorna."

"After that kiss," she said with the frankness that being a temporary siren allowed her, "I almost wish you were right."

His smile was no less attractive for being somewhat unwilling. "I am right. Count on it."

"No, Adam." She let herself go, let herself be the enchantress he saw when he looked in her eyes. "I've learned not to count on anything. It's a part of my nature, remember? I'm wild and I'm free and I live for the moment."

"There's a lot more to life, Lorna Smith," he answered quietly. "You'll miss the best part by always being on the run."

"And just what will I miss, Adam Gantry?"

"Commitment, steadiness, a firm hand in yours. Someone to turn to in the darkest hours of the night...."

"Shh." She put a finger against his full mouth. "No more. You might tempt me. And *I'm* the one who does the tempting around here, remember?"

His lips moved against her touch, but before he could form words, she shook her head and dropped her hand, turning to the car. She pulled open the door and slid in behind the wheel.

To distract herself from thoughts of the man who stood watching her through the side window, she set the practical side of her mind to ticking off the exigencies of the adventure ahead.

She needed a map to find her way to Prescott, Arizona. And somehow she needed to reach a man named Bucky O'Neill. She also had to get her suitcases and check out of the suite, but she couldn't do that until she'd safely shaken Adam. He'd be naturally suspicious if he had any hint of a sudden change of plans.

The pink leather upholstery held the scent of Astrid's perfume, and Lorna smiled to herself as she started the engine. Adam knocked on the window, and she rolled it down.

"You could save yourself a lot of trouble, just by being honest."

"Ah." She batted her eyelashes. "But what fun would that be?" She backed out of the space and headed for the exit ramp, sparing only a single regretful glance for the handsome, well-dressed man who watched her go. By the time he reached his own vehicle and tried to follow, she'd be long out of sight.

An hour later, she had her route mapped out, her suitcases in the trunk, and she was roaring down Interstate 10, on her way to the state highway that would lead her to Prescott.

The gently rolling desert that sped past on either side was dotted with the proud sentinels of saguaro cactus and the spiny, red-tipped blooms of ocotillo. The trip to Prescott, according to her map, would take around five hours. If all went well, she would be there by six o'clock. That should leave her enough time to find the mysterious Mr. O'Neill.

Lorna kept her eye on the temperature gauge, but so far it had stayed safely in the medium range. She went without the air conditioner, just to be on the safe side. Instead, she rolled the front windows down and turned on the radio and sang along to country and western songs while the hot desert wind whipped her hair around her face.

She'd crossed the border to Arizona and was almost to the State 60 turnoff when she realized that the burgundy Chrysler in her rearview mirror had been there for a long time. She slowed down and switched to a slower lane. The Chrysler did the same. She speeded up, and the Chrysler followed suit.

Utterly disgusted, she stuck her arm out the window and signaled the other car alongside the Cadillac. It slid smoothly into place and Adam rolled down the window and waved at her.

"I did see the words Prescott, Arizona, in that letter before you ate it," he shouted jauntily.

Lorna put her foot on the gas and left him behind. She turned the radio up full blast and sang at the top of her lungs and refused to decide whether she was ecstatic or upset that he hadn't given up.

Unfortunately, she forgot to watch the temperature gauge, and by the time she remembered to check it, she was barreling down State Highway 60 with nothing in sight for miles but cactus and sagebrush and the burgundy Chrysler that she couldn't seem to shake.

Four

———

Muttering an unladylike expletive under her breath,
Lorna pulled over onto the shoulder. She was afraid
to turn off the engine, having heard somewhere that
overheated cars should be allowed to cool down a bit
before being shut off.

She had either heard wrong or it was just too late for
letting the car idle to matter, because she could now
see steam escaping from under the hood.

As she considered her next move, the Chrysler slid
in behind her. Adam jumped out, sped to her driver's
door, and reaching in the open window, yanked the
keys from the ignition.

"I was just thinking I should do that myself." With
elaborate nonchalance, she studied a fingernail that
had been chipped in the tussle back at the hotel garage. In the desert silence, the car wheezed and

groaned like a winded moose. "Maybe we should look under the hood," she suggested after a moment.

"Maybe you want a few third-degree burns." He gave her a look so patronizing that she wished she had a large blunt object to hit him with. "You've got to let it cool down first, and then I'd have to predict that it won't be capable of taking you anywhere near where you want to go."

"I do adore your positive attitude."

He gave her one of those smiles that men give women when they have them where they want them. "It's still about a hundred miles to Prescott, and I imagine it's desert most of the way. This car won't get you there, I'm afraid."

"You don't sound very regretful."

"I suppose you'll have to ride with me."

She blew on her chipped fingernail. "I could just sit tight. Somebody else will come along."

"If you're lucky." Very neatly, he slid out of his suit jacket, slung it over his shoulders and proceeded to roll up his shirt cuffs. His tanned forearms had gold hairs on them. They looked very strong. Lorna decided he probably played tennis or squash at some exclusive L.A. club at least three times a week. "Whew," he said, really rubbing it in, "sure is hot out here."

He was putting it mildly. Without the whipping wind created by the speeding car, it was ninety degrees at least. Lorna's hair, which had slipped out of its loose confines completely, lay damp against her neck. She casually began stroking the tangled mass upward, repinning it as haphazardly as before. "I've always loved the heat," she purred. "It's so... sensual."

"Say that in an hour or two when your lips start cracking and your eyeballs go dry." Still behaving in an infuriatingly jaunty manner, he unknotted his tie and slid it from around his neck. Then he tossed the keys in the air and caught them. "Are your suitcases in the trunk?"

She said nothing. There was no need to. She was going to be stuck riding with him. He knew it, and she knew it. He strolled to the trunk of the car and transferred her bags to the Chrysler. Then he cheerfully tossed his coat and tie in the back seat and returned to where she sweltered behind the wheel of the wheezing Cadillac.

"Let's be on our way." He swung open her door.

"Could you please stop being so jovial? It's really getting on my nerves."

He reached for her hand and gently, but firmly, pulled her from the car. "Might as well make the best of an unpleasant situation."

"Might as well gloat a little, is what you mean."

He merely grinned in response. Then, pausing only to slip the Cadillac's keys beneath the floor mat, he led her to the Chrysler.

The interior of his car was marvelously cool. She settled into the leather seat with an internal sigh of contentment. Adam got in on his side and turned the engine over. The air conditioner hummed. Already, Lorna felt her clammy skin cooling.

"Please fasten your seat belt," a masculine voice issued from somewhere in the dashboard.

Lorna groaned. "Even your car likes giving orders." Adam granted her a forbearing glance. "All right, all right," she said, and did as the car had instructed.

They glided back out onto the sun-shimmered highway. In the rearview mirror, Lorna watched the Cadillac until it was only a speck of gleaming silver and pink. Then it disappeared.

Adam saw her watching the old car fade from sight. "I'll call for a tow truck," he said, picking up his car phone.

Lorna said nothing as Adam arranged to have the Cadillac towed back to Los Angeles where Astrid could reclaim it later. When he hung up, he made no more attempts at small talk. Apparently he felt complaisant now that he had the situation—and Lorna—firmly in hand. They drove on through the desert heat, enclosed in their little cocoon of cool air and mutual silence.

More than once, she glanced at his profile, so strong and determined-looking as he stared out through the tinted windshield at the flat road ahead. He must be tired. Chasing the elusive Astrid, he'd had no time for sleep in at least the past twenty-four hours. Still, he appeared utterly alert.

"Do you want me to drive for a while?" she suggested, her voice hesitant in the stillness between them. "You could take a nap."

He shot her a glance. "No, thanks. I'm fine."

"You mean you don't trust me."

"Partly."

"At least you're honest."

"Somebody around here has to be."

"I'm not even going to dignify that remark with a response."

"Glad to hear it." He spared her another jade-green glance. "Take a nap yourself if you want. It's still over an hour to Prescott."

"Maybe I will."

Lorna leaned her head back against the smooth leather and closed her eyes. The wheels whirred beneath her and the air conditioner hummed. After a while, she was vaguely aware that they were climbing, and that the road had more turns than before. She let her body roll with the movement of the car, not quite awake and not quite asleep.

When she opened her eyes again, they were surrounded by ponderosa pines. They had left the desert for national forest. Adam was resetting the clock as he drove.

"We lost an hour back there at the Arizona border," he explained. The digital display now read six-thirty.

Just then they passed the Prescott city limits sign. Adam pulled into the first gas station they came to and fueled up in the full service lane.

As the attendant took Adam's credit card, Lorna pushed open her door.

"Where do you think you're going?" Adam demanded.

"Even femme fatales have to visit the rest room occasionally," she replied sweetly. "Do you mind?"

"Just don't get any ideas. I'm right with you until we get to Astrid."

Lorna quietly closed the door in his face. She had to go into the station's convenience store to get the key from the gray-haired lady clerk. Adam actually got out of the car and stood right outside the glass door where he could see her. Then he stayed there while she went in the ladies' room a few feet away.

Lorna used the facilities, reapplied her lipstick and wondered how in the world she was going to ditch him again and also track down the mysterious Mr. O'Neill by ten o'clock. Still in the dark as to what to do next, she returned the key to the clerk, who looked at her rather oddly, she thought.

And why not? Excluding captured fugitives from justice, few grown women required an escort to go to the bathroom. Adam appeared oblivious to her disgusted grimace as she strode right past him. He followed close behind her back to the car.

"What now?" he asked, when they were both inside once more.

Good question, she answered silently. "Let's, um, just drive around town for a while, all right?"

"Where and what time are you meeting Astrid?"

"You are relentless."

"Where and when?"

Tossing him a quelling frown, Lorna did her best to remember the wording of Astrid's note, not easy since she hadn't exactly had time to study it in depth before being forced to eat it. It had said something like *visit Bucky O'Neill at ten tonight*, but there'd been absolutely no explanation as to how to find the man.

Could he be well known in Prescott? Perhaps some sort of local celebrity? Lorna stared blindly out her side window, thinking.

Just then, the clerk who'd watched her so suspiciously came out of the convenience store with the rest room key in her hand. Seeing her chance to question someone presumably from Prescott without her unswerving inquisitor listening in, Lorna just about leaped from the car.

"Where the hell are you going?" Adam was right behind her.

"Left my lipstick in the ladies' room," she tossed over her shoulder. She slipped around the white-painted metal door just as the clerk tried to shut it.

As the door closed and locked automatically, Lorna leaned against it. She found herself facing the single sink, and the wary clerk who'd backed against the wall between the towel dispenser and the gray plastic wastebasket.

"Don't be afraid. I just want to ask you a question," Lorna tried gamely.

The woman watched her, narrow-eyed over the rims of her bifocals. "You just step aside, miss, and let me out of here," she said.

Lorna tried a congenial smile. "It's not what you think. Really."

Adam rapped sharply on the door. "Lorna, this is pointless. You can't get out without going through me." His voice came through slightly muffled, but quite understandable.

"Out in a minute," she called back amiably, then she focused on the clerk again. "It's nothing illegal, I mean, I didn't *do* anything. He's just looking for his mother, and he thinks I know where she is.''

The steel door handle rattled. ''Lorna! Open this door.''

''Why don't you tell him, then?'' asked the clerk.

''She doesn't want to be found.''

''Lorna!''

''Settle down, young man!'' the clerk piped up. ''She'll be out in a minute!''

The door handle immediately stopped rattling. Silence came from outside the door.

Lorna and the clerk regarded each other. ''Thanks,'' Lorna said, then grinned again, sheepishly. ''He's now mortified. Your voice reminded him that he's made a fool of himself in public. Adam Gantry never makes a fool of himself.''

The clerk grinned back. ''Know him that well, do you?''

''We met this morning.''

''Love at first sight?''

''No. He's not my type at all.''

The clerk made a humphing sound in response to that. Then she asked, ''Now what's your question?''

''Oh, right.'' Lorna lowered her voice, to make sure it wouldn't travel to listening ears outside. ''Have you ever heard of a man named Bucky O'Neill?''''

The woman grunted. ''Maybe I didn't go to college, but I do know my history.''

''History?''

''Captain William Bucky O'Neill. Of the Rough Riders. Fought in the war with Spain.''

Lorna gulped. ''The Spanish-American War?''

"You bet."

"But that was back at the turn of the century. That would make Bucky O'Neill—"

"Dead," the woman said with finality. "He died in the war. He was a hero."

Lorna let out a long breath. Now what? she thought. Visit Bucky O'Neill indeed. Was Astrid playing some kind of joke on her? If so, Lorna didn't get it.

The woman went on. "We've even got a statue dedicated to him. Over in the town square on Gurley."

Lorna had let herself slump against the door. Now she snapped to attention. "A statue? Of Bucky O'Neill." The joke was starting to make sense.

The woman shifted from one foot to the other. "You bet. Now, is that all you wanted to know?"

"The statue. Where is it?"

"Just keep going on the road you're on, to the center of town. Courthouse Square at Gurley and Marina. Can't miss it." The clerk was beginning to look uncomfortable. "Now, if you don't mind..."

"Oh. Oh, yes. Sorry." Lorna pulled the door open, then paused to look back at the clerk one last time. "Thank you."

"No problem." She winked. "And good luck with that man who isn't your type at all."

The door closed behind her and Lorna found herself face-to-face with a little over six feet worth of annoyed male. Adam immediately captured her arm and began herding her toward his car. "That was a ridiculous thing to do, Lorna. I'm running out of patience."

Lorna dug in her heels. "So am I. Let go of my arm." Surprisingly, he did. She took that small victory over his recent dominance of her and ran with it. "I appreciate your giving me a lift here. But now I can fend for myself. I want my things out of your trunk now, please."

"Lorna, don't be childish."

"I am not being childish, Adam Gantry. I'm an adult who has a perfect right to go where she wants when she wants with whomever she wants. And I don't want to go anywhere else with you. Is that clear enough? Now please get my things from your trunk."

"I'm not going to go away," he said grimly.

"We'll see. Now, open your trunk."

Short of using physical force, there wasn't much more he could do. He opened the trunk for her and set the suitcases near the phone kiosk where she instructed him to. Then he got in the car and started it up. Lorna couldn't believe he was giving in so easily, and she was right. He wasn't. He was only moving the car out of the fill-up lane. He pulled in right beside her suitcases and sat there, glowering, while she called a taxi.

The Ace City cab arrived in minutes. After she and her suitcases were safely inside, she asked for a hotel near Courthouse Square.

"Ma'am, do you know there's a guy following us?" the cabby asked as they jockeyed through the light early-evening traffic.

Lorna turned and glanced at Adam's car. "Unfortunately, yes. Ignore him."

"Oh, it's like that," the cabby said knowingly.

Lorna shrugged and looked out the window. Within minutes, she was deposited at the Hassayampa Inn, a splendid modified Spanish structure of ruffled brick in shades of deep red and blue. Copper cornices gleamed in the fading sunlight, and the trim was white, with plaster medallions set at intervals near the tile roof.

Lorna admired the architecture and ignored the Chrysler that slid in right behind the cab. "What a lovely old hotel," she said to the driver.

A uniformed bellman appeared and loaded her bags onto a cart.

"You're lucky it's May," the cabdriver said. "In June and July it's hard to find a last-minute vacancy in this town." He pointed across the street. "And there's the square. In walking distance, like you wanted."

Lorna handed him the metered amount plus a generous tip. Then she entered the doors of the hotel. She checked into a small but beautifully appointed room on the second floor and went back to the lobby after getting rid of her suitcases. Adam dogged her every step.

She strolled unconcernedly out onto Marina Street. She would have to find a way to lose him, but right now he had no way of knowing she was on a foray to scout out the location where Astrid would contact her.

Courthouse Square was a place of maple trees and thick green grass. The statue of Bucky O'Neill on a spirited horse reared up at the toe-end of a horseshoe-shaped walk into which was set a time line of important events in Prescott history. Aware every moment of the man who dogged her steps, Lorna made a great show of reading the tiles set into the walk.

At the statue itself, she stopped and slowly let her gaze travel upward. The plaque at the base declared it one of the finest equestrian monuments in the world, and Lorna did find it beautiful, the powerful rearing horse and its Rough Rider, all action and excitement cast forever in rich bronze.

She studied her immediate surroundings. Trees. Grass. The horseshoe-shaped walk. Benches. A gazebo not far away. The big stone courthouse loomed behind the statue. To her right lay Gurley Street and a mailbox and a set of phone kiosks. Behind her was Marina Street and the Hassayampa Inn.

She fervently hoped this was the place.

Well, she told herself, if it wasn't she'd find out at ten o'clock.

Now to get rid of Adam....

He'd taken a seat on a nearby bench. She decided, rather regretfully, that the best way to shake him would be to deceive him again, to let him think she'd given in to his refusal to leave her alone and then, later, nearer the appointed time, to slip away when he least suspected it.

She turned and, very slowly, strolled toward him. He watched her, his green gaze wary.

"You're not going to give up, are you?" she asked when she stood looking down at him.

"No." He was facing the sun, which hung heavy in the western sky above the pine-blanketed hills. He shaded his eyes with his arm. "Just tell me when and where."

"I'm starving," she said, and held out her hand. "Let's eat."

Shaking his head, smiling in spite of himself, he grasped her outstretched palm. Once again, she felt that curling warmth at his touch, and she let her mouth curve into a come-hither smile. It felt so good, to be utterly free for the first time in her life and to be touching someone who made her feel as reckless as a Rough Rider on a powerful stallion.

Adam was squinting at her, against the red ball of the sun. "You won't tempt me off my guard again," he said. His voice had that delicious roughness that made her want to rub herself against it.

"The lady in the hotel lobby said that's Whiskey Row over there." She pointed toward Gurley Street. "After dark, all those bars open and every one of them has a band. I'm going to eat, Adam. And then I'm going dancing. Want to come?"

He grunted. She laughed, pulled him to his feet and led him back to the hotel.

The boutique in the lobby was open, so she made him wait while she bought some of the bright new clothes she'd promised herself, including a pair of white cowboy boots and a bag to match, some tight red jeans, a silky camisole top and a rawhide jacket with plenty of fringe. She modeled the clothes for him, twirling between the blue velvet chair where he sat and a long dressing mirror.

"It's exactly your style," he gave out grudgingly after a moment. His voice tried to be condescending, but she saw the heat in his eyes as his gaze unwillingly traveled up the formfitting line of the crimson jeans.

She turned to the clerk. "I think I'll wear this outfit now," she said. The clerk agreed to have the other new clothes, as well as the ones she'd been wearing, returned to her room.

After a quick trip to Adam's car where he once again donned his coat, they ate in the hotel dining room which lay beyond Peacock Alley, a hallway tiled in peacock blue, of which the hotel was justly proud.

Lorna ordered a nice big bottle of Chardonnay, but Adam refused to touch it. Adam watched her chatter happily through the meal, while he chewed the excellent food stolidly, looking as if he couldn't afford to relax his guard for a split second.

It was near nine o'clock when they finished eating. "Now, we go dancing," she announced, once they stood beneath the plaster medallions in front of the old hotel.

She pranced off down the street toward the music that could already be heard on nearby Gurley. Out of the corner of her eye, she noted the rearing shadow of Bucky O'Neill in the night-lighted square. Somehow, she had to get rid of Adam and be waiting beneath the bronze horse's hoofs within the hour.

When they reached Whiskey Row, Lorna's hopes of leaving her escort behind rose considerably. Though it had seemed just an ordinary commercial street in the daylight, on Saturday night the place clearly came alive. Already, good-natured partiers jostled each other as they went from club to club. If luck was with her, within the hour the crowds would really thicken. It would be easy to lose Adam in the crush and sneak across the street.

Dragging Adam behind her, she followed a group of revelers dressed in shiny boots and spotless hats into the Palace, the first saloon that struck her fancy.

Beyond the long, crowded bar the big room inside opened up to a pine-paneled dance hall. The band at the far wall played fast country music while couples two-stepped and a few adventurous souls practiced the intricate footwork of a line dance across the wooden floor.

High tables and a few stools along the wall provided a place to watch the action. Lorna quickly claimed a rare clear space and hoisted herself up on the stool. Adam, looking completely out of place in his expensive suit, stood right beside her. His expression defined the word stoic.

A waitress in jeans and a tank top asked what they'd have.

Adam shook his head. Lorna ordered a strawberry daiquiri and heard Adam's knowing snort.

The waitress left them. "What was that supposed to mean?" Lorna demanded.

He moved in a little closer, so they could talk while the band played. "What?"

"That *noise* you made when I ordered my drink."

He shrugged. "Nothing. I just knew you were going to order something pink with an umbrella in it."

She slipped out of her fringed jacket and tossed it across the little table in front of her. More than one set of masculine eyes took a slow walk over her bare, gleaming shoulders in the skimpy camisole.

"Put that jacket back on," Adam said impassively.

"Why?"

He snared the soft leather and draped it over her shoulders. "Let's just say there's a draft in here."

Her pink drink arrived. She took a quick sip and then slid off the stool. "I want to dance, Adam. And with you standing there looking like my keeper, no one's going to dare ask me." Defiantly, she slipped the jacket from her shoulders once again and tossed it on the table. "So it looks like you'll have to do for a partner—or would you rather I pulled a Sadie Hawkins and did the asking myself?"

Apparently, he preferred taking her in his arms to letting her two-step out of his reach with some obliging cowboy. He led her out on the wooden floor.

The band played a slow song. Around them, the other couples shifted into a slower, more intimate rhythm, their bodies moving close to one another. Adam, true to form, assumed a rigid ballroom stance. You could have wedged a beach ball between his cordovan belt and Lorna's denim waistband.

As always seemed to happen when she touched him, Lorna felt her pulse pick up. And she felt that naughtiness, that wildness that was so unlike her real self, come all the more to the fore. Something about all the control Adam exhibited inspired her to give her all to break it down.

In a smooth, slithery movement, she circled his neck with both hands and brought her body up against his.

"Lorna," he said. It was supposed to be a reprimand, but the huskiness in his voice betrayed him.

His body was so nice and solid. Pressing against him made her feel secure, and yet excited. She lifted her head and tipped her face up to his. "I've changed my mind, about your name," she said.

He looked down at her, saying nothing, his golden brows drawn together in a questioning expression.

"Maybe the Gantry does fit after all. Maybe there's some dashingness way down inside you that you haven't quite been able to extinguish, like an ember that just won't die. A sleeping spark."

"Next you'll be telling me it's your mission to fan that ember to a flame." His voice was rueful, bordering dangerously on tender.

She traced little figure eights on the back of his neck with one oval fingernail. "I wish..."

"Go on."

That just once in my life a man would look at the *real* me the way you're looking at me now. Her mind whispered the words, but of course she didn't say them.

"Hey, why so sad suddenly?" He was tipping her chin up so she looked in his eyes once again.

"Oh, Adam..."

His fingers slid backward, cupping her neck beneath the wild spill of her hair, cradling her face in a grip that was at once achingly sensual and full of gentle understanding. "You can tell me."

"No." A single traitorous tear welled over and trailed down her cheek. He brushed at it, in a stunningly compassionate caress, with the pad of his thumb. "I'm sorry, Adam. I just can't."

Miraculously, he seemed to accept her refusal to confide in him. He pulled her head against his broad chest and held it there, saying no more. She listened to the steady, reassuring beat of his heart, her sadness fading as the dance came to its inevitable conclusion.

As a fast number began again, he led the way for once, pulling her back to the little table. He scooped up her jacket, draped it on her shoulders, and headed for the door, still firmly holding her hand.

"Where are we going?" she asked, struggling to get the jacket on, as they passed the long bar and went out into the brightly lit, crowded street.

"Somewhere quiet," he tossed the words back over his shoulder as he pulled her along.

He plowed through the crowds. "No, wait, I want to dance some more." He ignored her protests, and Lorna knew why. She sounded totally unconvincing. The emotions that had surfaced in the Palace had somewhat dampened her party spirits.

"We'll go across the street," he said, not pausing in his purposeful stride. "There are a few benches by that statue."

Lorna had to restrain herself from groaning aloud. Without knowing it, he was planning to drag her right to the place where Astrid would be contacting her in—she darted a glance at her watch—twenty-five minutes.

"No, Adam!" She stopped stock-still just before they reached the corner, and jerked her hand from his grasp. She shoved the hand into the other arm of the fringed jacket, which she'd been only half wearing as he towed her down the street.

He turned to her. "What's the matter now?"

"I, um, came here to dance, and I'm going to have a good time."

People milled around them, but Adam ignored them completely. "Lorna, be honest with yourself for once. You were upset in there. You need to deal with it. The time comes when the party has to end, and you have to face the things that are really bothering you."

Saying nothing in response, Lorna turned and walked away, around the corner, down the darkened side street in the opposite direction from the park and the hotel. Behind the corner building, there was a small parking lot rimmed by a low brick retaining wall. Lorna sat on the low wall and stared down at her new white boots.

Slowly, Adam came after her. He sat beside her.

For a time, neither spoke. Muted on the night air came the cacophony of sounds from the bands and milling throngs around the corner.

Lorna debated with herself. She was tired of running, tired of trying to keep one step ahead of the relentless man beside her. He'd been so tender, so understanding in those few moments on the dance floor, that she was having second thoughts about keeping him from Astrid.

When you came right down to it, she found herself reasoning, Astrid had never said a word about her own problems when she'd appeared at Lorna's hotel room last night. It wasn't as if Astrid had actually asked Lorna to keep her whereabouts a secret. Last night, Astrid hadn't even *mentioned* her son—let alone the man she'd left waiting at their engagement party.

And it wasn't as if Adam were some kind of monster, after all. He was truly concerned about his mother, about her welfare and her future, and that was why he was being so overbearingly persistent about finding her.

Why not, Lorna wondered, let mother and son settle this problem between themselves? Why not step aside and let them handle their family matters without her interference?

She cast him an oblique glance. He looked calm and unruffled as always, sitting beside her on the low brick wall.

"Ready to talk about it?" he asked.

"Do you realize you haven't asked me where or when I'm meeting your mother in at least two hours?"

A smile played on his lips. "Asking you hasn't been terribly successful up to this point. And besides, I think if you start being honest with me, you might be honest about everything, including where I can find Astrid."

Not everything, she thought, her emotions equal parts defiance and sadness. Because I can't help it, Adam. I love the way you look at me. It's just what I need right now, to know a man sees me as everything sexy and feminine and dangerous that there is in the world. I want to go on feeling like that, for a little bit longer, just a little bit more....

"All right." Lorna stood up. "Let's go."

"Where to?"

"You want a chance to talk to Astrid, don't you?"
He stood up beside her. "Lead the way."

Five

"Astrid said she would contact you here at ten, and that's all?" Adam asked.

"The letter said to visit Bucky O'Neill and she'd contact me there. Since the man's been dead for almost a century, this statue was the closest I could come."

They were sitting on a bench a few feet from the statue in question. It was five minutes to ten.

"I still don't get it, Lorna. Can you tell me now what the hell is going on?"

She looked at him levelly. "Adam, I really don't know."

It was the truth, when she came right down to it. She had no idea what was driving Astrid. As for her own actions, it was as if another, totally different woman had come alive inside her. And the old Lorna often had no inkling what the new Lorna would do next.

"It's something to do with that group you two belong to, isn't it? They're manipulating you both and you've taken a vow of secrecy."

"Adam, for a solid citizen, you certainly have a vivid imagination."

"I'm concerned about my mother." He captured her glance. "And heaven help me, I'm starting to feel the same way about you."

"Concerned, you mean?"

"Yes."

She assumed a pose of bad-girl bravado. "Don't be. I can take care of myself."

He shook his head. "Your life's a mess. Look at you. It's obvious you don't even know day to day where you'll lay your head at night. What about your job—do you have a job?"

"Yes."

"Is your boss holding it for you until you decide to come to work again?"

"I'm on vacation, Adam. And I own my own business, anyway."

"What kind of business?"

She thought of her bookstore, of the neat rows of shelves labeled Fiction and Nonfiction, History and Psychology, Gardening and Art. He'd never for a moment believe her if she told him that bad Lorna Smith owned a bookstore in Westwood, usually wore her hair in a bun, and preferred PBS to commercial television.

"I'm in communications," she said.

"Lorna—"

She didn't let him continue. "Look. You wanted to talk to Astrid. That's what we're here for. If you want to be concerned about something, why don't you worry if this is the right place at all, and if she'll even show her face once she sees that you're here?"

"All right, Lorna. If that's how you want it." He sounded so infinitely patient and sympathetic that she once again felt the wild Lorna taking over.

If it was Adam Gantry's mission to save bad Lorna Smith, she thought, then maybe it was naughty Lorna's calling to let the air out of his stuffed shirt.

She nimbly scrambled to her knees on the bench and put her mouth against his ear. "If I told you how I *really* want it, would you give it to me just that way?"

She heard his sharp indrawn breath as he turned his head toward her, pulling back at the same time, like a man scenting danger, facing it, but claiming distance.

And then he smiled. "You *are* bad." Wisely, he didn't answer her question. "And, all right, we'll change the subject."

She resumed a more decorous position on the bench. "Thank you."

They waited in silence as the minutes crawled past.

"It's ten after ten," he said.

Lorna shrugged, wondering wistfully how her Mercedes was holding up. "As I said before, I'm not even sure this is the right place."

Just then, the phone in one of the kiosks across the lawn by the sidewalk rang. For a split second, their gazes locked. And then Adam was up and sprinting across the grass.

Since she was too late to get there before he did anyway, Lorna followed at a more sedate pace.

"Just what the hell is going on?" she heard Adam demanding into the mouthpiece in an intense, low voice as she came up beside him on the sidewalk. "Tell me where you are."

Lorna stepped back, turning away, to let Adam have some privacy as he spoke with his mother.

His voice rose. "Astrid, be reasonable. I'm concerned about you. Listen, whatever it is, tell me. Let me help you—" Suddenly, he stopped arguing. For a moment, he said nothing. Then, "If you'll just—all right. Don't hang up. All right." His tone held total resignation.

"She wants to talk to you," he said.

Lorna took the receiver.

"Hello, Sister," a low, throaty voice said in her ear. "Better let me do the talking, okay?"

Lorna made a small noise of agreement.

"My goodness, darlin'," Astrid went on, "I'm sorry about this. Believe me, I would have told you my own situation if I'd thought Adam would have any way to track me down. I'm just a little stunned, to tell the truth. I need some time to rethink this thing—your Mercedes is fine, by the way. Is the Caddy holding up okay?"

"It died in the desert," Lorna said flatly.

"Oh, no. But you managed anyway."

"Adam was there."

"Well." An airy sigh came from the other end of the line. "Whatever works."

Lorna cupped her hand over the receiver and whispered, so the nearby and glowering Adam couldn't make out what she said. "What now, Astrid?" Her low tone was as grim as the words.

"I need to think."

"Would you mind thinking fast?"

"Okay. Look. I'll be in touch again tomorrow morning, say seven o'clock. The Boca Grande Café in Winslow. I know you could probably strangle me by now, but if you would just . . ."

Astrid's voice trailed off, as if she couldn't quite bring herself to ask so much. Lorna realized that it was Astrid's turn to need reassurance.

"Anything," Lorna said firmly. "Just tell me."

"Keep Adam with you until I decide what I should do, but don't let him come with you to the café in the morning." Lorna was silent. "I know, he's persistent," Astrid went on.

"That's putting it mildly," Lorna remarked.

"Do you think you can handle it?"

A few feet away, Adam was eyeing her suspiciously. "Mission accepted," she said into the receiver.

"Thanks, pal," said the husky voice in her ear. "Tomorrow, then." The line went dead.

"Where is she?" Adam asked the question in a monotone, as if he felt obliged to do so, though he knew he'd get no satisfactory answer.

"She didn't say." Lorna almost hated herself for having no more to tell him than what he expected. She added after a wordless moment, "I have to go."

"Where?"

"I—"

"I know. You can't tell me."

She let her answer be found in her silence.

"I'll have to rent a car," she said, as if talking to herself.

"No you won't," he said, as she'd known he would. "I'll take you."

She shook her head, knowing she mustn't go along too easily. She thought, deception upon deception, and wondered where and how it would end. She was going to have to ditch him briefly in the morning, and it was important that he have no clue of when or where she might do that. Keeping him totally in the dark as to what she was up to seemed the only way she'd have a chance of getting him to let down his guard at the appropriate time.

Unfortunately, everything she *didn't* say was bound to make him more sure that she and his mother were being manipulated by some mysterious cult of man-hating women.

"It's late to try to get a car," he argued reasonably.

She pretended to consider. "I really couldn't tell you anything, Adam. You'd just have to go where I asked you to take me."

"Fine," he said.

"Does that mean you'll stop the unending questions?"

"That means I'll take you wherever you want to go. I'm *not* going to give up trying to find out what the hell's going on. Promising I will would be a lie." He gave her a chiding frown and added, "I've always detested lies."

His dig hit her where it hurt. The real Lorna Smith prided herself on her scrupulous honesty. But somehow the naughty Lorna seemed to spend all her time rearranging the truth to suit her own needs.

Across the street, the bands played on. Lorna tapped her foot to a drumbeat that pounded louder than the rest.

"You detest lies," she tossed at him, her hostility a product of her guilt. "So you're saying you detest me, right? Because you think I'm lying."

"I know you're lying. But no, I don't detest you, Lorna."

His tone of extreme forbearance set her teeth on edge. Not even for Astrid's sake, she thought, could she put up with this.

"Forget it." She spun on her heel. "I'll get my own transportation."

He was beside her within three steps, catching her arm, and whirling her around to face him. "All right. I promise I'll *try* to stop asking questions."

She pulled her arm from his grip. "It won't work. You know it, I know it. You're not going to give up until I lead you to Astrid."

He grunted. And then he smiled. "You still need a ride tonight. And I'm still available."

Enchanted once again by the charm and humor that lurked beneath his facade of puritanical self-control, she replied, "Let me get my things."

There were two roads that would take them to Interstate 40 and eventually to Winslow. Lorna chose Highway 89, which seemed the most direct. The road wove through the mountains and down into the desert again.

As they left the trees behind and the land opened up before them, Lorna stared silently out the window, mesmerized by the austere beauty of the desert world that fled by on either side. By the silvering light of the waning moon, the dry earth seemed to roll on forever, dotted here and there with clumps of sagebrush, proud saguaros and the tortured shadows of joshua trees. She did her best to simply appreciate the stark scenery and not to even try to figure out how she was going to evade the man beside her when morning came.

They began climbing again, up into the gray-green stands of ponderosa pines. By midnight, they reached the interstate and sped on to Flagstaff. There, she made Adam stop at a phone booth where she pretended to place a call.

"I have to be in New Mexico by noon tomorrow," she said when she rejoined Adam at the car. It was a total fabrication, meant to throw him off guard.

"Where in New Mexico?" he asked, taken in.

She shook her head. "You know I can't say."

He took the map from the floor of the car and spread it out on the hood. "It's less than two hundred miles to the New Mexico border," he said. "Why don't we call it a night here in Flagstaff and try for a few hours' sleep? We can get an early start and—"

She shook her head again. "Let's go a little farther, okay? We're still too far away for me to feel comfortable stopping."

He shrugged. "You know where you're going." She pretended not to notice the irony in his words as she settled back into the passenger seat.

They drove on through the deepening night, past towns named Winona and Two Guns, right by the turnoff that could have taken them to Meteor Crater. In spite of the lateness of the hour, Lorna felt her imagination stirring.

On the road ahead, there would be hundreds of turnoffs to choose from. And each one would bring its own special kind of adventure. And that, in the end, was what she was after. Adventure. A change in her perspective, a new way of looking at the world. And if she thought of recent events in that light, well, she was getting just what she wanted. Just because Adam insisted too often on being a harbinger of gloom didn't mean she had to be gloomy right along with him.

She was flushed with a new resolve to keep things light and upbeat when they reached Winslow.

Lorna stretched, elaborately, and said, "All right. Let's find someplace to sleep."

Winslow's two main streets, called Second and Third, were each one-way, so Adam ended up navigating a circle while Lorna pretended to look for a suitable place. In actuality, she was watching for the Boca Grande Café, which they passed not too far from the freeway on Second Street.

She waited until they were parallel the café on Third Street, before settling on the Super Duper Motel. One block over and two blocks up and she'd be at the café in the morning. It would be a nominal distance, even on foot.

Though the Super Duper Motel itself was distinctly *un*distinctive, boasting forty rooms on two floors, each opening on the parking lot, Lorna found its upbeat name appealing.

When they pulled up to the office, Adam turned to her. "One room, all right?"

No way, she thought. One room would be too dangerously intimate, let alone making it all the harder to get away in the morning.

But then she reconsidered. The naughty Lorna would never quibble about anything so trivial as sharing a room with a man she was attracted to. Saying no would be out of character. He'd become doubly suspicious. His guard would be up and she'd never escape him in the morning.

She smiled at him—tauntingly, she hoped. "Hm. One room. Is that a proposition?"

"Don't worry." His voice was flat. "I'll get separate beds."

She tried a teasing smile, wishing vainly for one in return. "But do you snore?"

"No," he said. His face remained impassive.

Sighing, Lorna put her hand on his arm. "Adam. Let's lighten it up a little, okay? I mean, we're in this situation together and we might as well make the best of it."

"Right," he said, and went in to the motel office to register for their room.

The room had two double beds with worn red chenille bedspreads. The television was bolted to its stand and water could be heard dripping in the bathroom sink.

"Charming," Lorna said. "I especially like the drapes. They look like modern art from the brush of a crazed orangutan."

"You chose it," Adam muttered.

"All right if I use the bathroom first?" she asked, insolently cheerful.

"Go ahead."

Lorna closed the door behind her, engaging the privacy lock.

As Adam heard the sound of water running in the sink, he smiled grimly to himself. The opportunity to uncover a little of the mystery of Lorna Smith was now at hand. She'd taken one full-size suitcase and her overnight case into the bathroom with her. But the white shoulder bag that she'd bought to match her new boots sat waiting on the vanity counter by the bathroom door.

Adam avoided meeting his own eyes in the mirror as he unzipped the little purse. Pawing through another's belongings offended his moral sense of right and wrong. However, in this case, he didn't see what else he could do. So he ignored the nagging of his conscience as he spread out a hand towel to muffle the sound and dumped the purse's contents on the counter.

He discovered immediately that she was carrying a substantial sum of traveller's checks and several major credit cards.

Her driver's license said she was almost thirty and just who she claimed to be. The picture of her, though, made him stop and stare for precious seconds. It was a plain, unadorned version of the Lorna he knew. As if she'd scrubbed her face clean and raked her hair back to take her driver's test. He couldn't help smiling at it. She looked so wary and vulnerable that way.

In an accordion strip of photo windows, she carried studio portraits of three babies and a little girl in pigtails. She also had three snapshots, one of a gray-haired couple and the others of two very pretty women. By the obvious physical resemblances, he assumed that the older couple were Lorna's parents and the two women either cousins or sisters. They were all very wholesome-looking, with their attractive faces and friendly smiles. He imagined Lorna must be the black sheep.

He stood for a few moments, staring at the pictures, wondering about her childhood and about how she'd grown up. But then the water stopped running in the other room, and he realized he should get on with it.

He opened her business-card case. On ivory parchment stock, her cards announced that she was the proprietress of The Book Nook, used and hard-to-find books being her specialty.

I own my own business, she'd told him. Was that actually the truth, then? Or was she just outrageous enough to have business cards printed for a make-believe concern?

Now, he decided, was no time to ponder that question.

Swiftly, Adam pocketed one business card and jotted down her home address from her driver's license. Then he shoveled the contents back into her purse and set it just where Lorna had left it. He shook out the towel and hung it back on the rack.

He considered chancing a phone call, but decided against it. She'd be through in the bathroom any minute. Besides, the detective he needed to contact would be hard to reach at one in the morning on Saturday night, and this was hardly a situation where Adam could leave a number to call back.

Intrigued with the information he'd uncovered, Adam stretched out on one of the beds and tried to make himself relax. He knew, however, that relaxation was unlikely, in spite of the deep-breathing exercises his fitness trainer had taught him.

Plagued as he was by insomnia, it was often difficult for him to get a full night's sleep even under ideal conditions. Tonight, in a strange and lumpy bed, worried about Astrid, and wondering what wild thing Lorna Smith would do next, sleep was not even an option.

Not that he wanted it to be. No, he was better off wide-awake and ready for action. Around Lorna Smith, that was the only way to keep up.

In the bathroom, Lorna donned one of the more modest gowns from her wedding trousseau, a slinky ivory silk that covered her from low neckline to ankles, but clung a little more provocatively than might be appropriate. The peignoir that went with it disguised a few more of her curves, but made what didn't show all the more enticing.

She shook her head at herself in the cracked mirror. No, poor Adam would expire of grimness if she emerged from the bathroom dressed like this. He'd be sure she was out to ravish him.

She dropped the slinky silk to the floor and foraged around in her opened suitcase, finally coming up with a huge white T-shirt with a pink unicorn printed on the front that had been a gift from her eight-year-old niece.

The T-shirt would have to do. She slipped it over her head and the hem fell halfway to her knees.

"Done?" Adam asked absently when she rejoined him in the main room. He was stretched out on one of the red-covered beds, reading a brochure that had been left on the nightstand.

"Your turn."

Still not looking at her, he swung his feet off the bed, and reached for the little overnight kit he'd taken from his trunk. "I'm going to shower," he announced. "A long, hot shower."

"Good idea," she said.

He disappeared in the bathroom, significantly taking his car keys from the top of the television as he went by. After a few minutes, she heard the shower running.

Lorna set her travel clock for 5:00 a.m., thinking that would give her two hours to get away from Adam. Then she slid beneath the covers of the other bed, and switched out the lamp on her side. She plumped her two flat pillows and thought vaguely of turning on the television, seeing what the late-night viewing was like in Winslow. But there was no remote, and she would have had to get up to do it. She was just tired enough that the bed seemed almost comfortable, and before she was even aware she was sleepy, her eyes were drooping closed.

Lorna had no idea what woke her in the deepest part of the night. A glance at her travel clock told her it was 3:00 a.m. Fitfully, she turned over to face Adam's side of the room.

He'd turned off his light. The room lay in deep shadow, the only illumination was that which bled through the ugly drapes from the garish motel sign out front, but she could make out his shape. He was sitting up against the headboard. His chest was bare and the covers were pulled up to his waist.

"Adam?"

"Go back to sleep."

"Adam, what is it?"

"There's nothing wrong. Go back to sleep."

"Did you sleep at all?"

"I'm fine."

She sat up and turned on her light, squinting against the sudden glare. Then she rubbed her eyes and turned to him. He still sat against the headboard, his expression grim, his bare, well-muscled chest covered with a light dusting of hairs the same golden color as his eyebrows.

"Turn off the light. Go back to sleep," he said.

"Adam, I know you didn't sleep last night. You need some rest."

"I'm fine."

"You keep saying that, through clenched teeth. It's not very convincing. Aren't you tired?"

"I want to keep an eye on you."

"Eventually, you have to sleep."

"That's what you think." He uttered the words so bleakly that she had a sudden urge to throw back her covers and go to him.

She stopped herself. "What do you mean?" she asked cautiously.

"I mean I have trouble sleeping, that's all. No big mystery."

"You mean like insomnia?"

"Yes."

"But don't they have treatments for that. Sleep clinics, that sort of thing?"

He spoke defensively. "I saw a therapist about it."

"And?"

"He said that in my case it appeared to be a problem of control. When I sleep, I have to relinquish control. And I'm not good at that."

Something welled up inside her—a soft little ache. Lorna recognized the emotion: tenderness. Here was this big, strong, domineering man, and he was scared to death to let himself be vulnerable enough to get a good night's sleep.

"How long has it been, since you slept?"

"I've slept," he said, sounding like a recalcitrant little boy.

"Just answer the question, Adam."

"I slept for five hours Wednesday night."

"You haven't slept the past two nights?" she murmured disbelievingly. "Not at all?"

"I've gone longer. Believe me."

"But it's *bad* for you, not to have your rest."

"Lorna, no one ever died from insomnia. Think about it. When you finally get tired enough, you go to sleep."

"But how long does that take?"

"I went for over a week once."

"That's awful." It suddenly occurred to her that his grim behavior since they had checked into the motel was probably directly related to his inability to sleep. He knew bedtime was coming, and he knew he was going to spend the night staring at the wall.

"Turn off your light and go back to sleep. It's nothing to be upset about," he said after a moment.

Lorna tossed back the red spread and stood up. "Turn over," she said. "And lie on your stomach."

His glance flicked over her bare legs and the huge shirt and settled on her sleep-flushed face. "Get back in that bed."

She folded her arms and frowned obdurately. "Turn over. I'm going to give you a massage."

"I'm not in the mood for games, Lorna."

"Neither am I. You need to relax, whether you think you can go to sleep or not. A massage will relax you." He stared at her, warily. She showed him her hands, palms up. "Adam, please. I'm just trying to help."

"You mean that," he said after a pregnant silence. It was a statement, not a question.

"Yes. Please let me help you."

"I'll never fall asleep, so you'll be wasting your time. Especially if you're thinking you'll sneak out while I'm unconscious."

"Come on. I'm not your prisoner, and we both know it. I can walk out that door any time I want, whether you're asleep or not."

"But if I'm asleep, I can't follow you."

"Look. How about if I promise not to run out on you?" Or if I do, it'll only be for a little while, she added silently.

He was regarding her skeptically from under lowered brows.

"I would never break a promise, Adam," she said quietly, "no matter what you may think of me." She strode purposefully to the vanity counter, feeling Adam's gaze boring through her back the whole time. She took a tube of lotion from her overnight case.

When she turned to him again, he was still sitting against the headboard, frowning. She walked toward him, trying to look brisk and no-nonsense, like a nurse with a difficult patient.

He looked up at her. "You only want to help me, do you?" That husky undertone had come into his voice.

Standing there, her bare feet chilled on the threadbare motel carpet, Lorna Smith clutched her tube of lotion and examined her motives. Silently, she admitted that her motives were mixed. She shifted her gaze to the velvet painting of a big-eyed child on the wall above the headboard.

Yes, I want to help you, she thought. And I also want you to be sound asleep when I go to meet Astrid in the morning. And, beyond that . . . She caught her lower lip between her teeth as she admitted to herself, I want to touch you. . . .

"You can answer any time," he prompted.

She forced herself to look at him, and as soon as she did it, she realized she never wanted to look away. He was so beautiful. His chest was strong and deep, the cords of muscles in his arms powerfully defined. The gold hairs on his skin looked crisp and inviting to the touch. Her fingers itched to trail down his flat belly, where the hairs disappeared beneath the red bedspread. She realized that a man in his thirties with a sedentary job didn't keep a body like that without a great amount of hard work and self-discipline. And, of course, if there was one thing Adam Gantry had in excess, it was discipline.

His discipline was part of what attracted her so strongly. The Lorna she had been until the night before admired it. And the new, naughty Lorna longed to make him lose it completely, at least for the night.

Lorna gulped. "You're right." She saluted him with the tube of lotion. "Bad idea. I'll just get back in my own bed." She started to turn.

His hand shot out and closed on her wrist. The warm, firm touch sent a hot little shiver clear down to her chilled toes. She looked into his eyes.

"You never did answer my question," he said.

"No, and I'm not going to now."

For some inexplicable reason, that seemed to satisfy him. He released her and rolled onto his stomach, keeping the red spread up at his trim waist. "I'd appreciate a massage," he said in a neutral tone. "You're right. It'll make me less tense, if nothing else."

Six

Lorna gulped again, wishing the lump that kept rising in her throat would stay down. She stared at the golden-brown expanse of Adam's muscled back and shoulders. Where to begin?

She considered perching on the edge of the bed, but that would have her rubbing from the side, not nearly as effective as a more direct angle would be.

Holding onto the tube of lotion as if it were a lifeline, she hoisted a bare knee up onto the side of his bed, and then swung the other leg over him, so she came to rest astraddle his waist and the hard curve of his masculine buttocks.

"Am I too heavy?" she asked, hoping he didn't notice the breathy break in her voice.

"You're fine." He tossed the pillows to the floor and slid his sculpted arms up and out, bent at the elbow, so that his hands were parallel with his head. She assumed that was to give her easier access to the various muscle groups.

The knot in her throat was still there. She forced it down once again and squeezed some lotion into her palm. She rubbed her hands together, preparatory to beginning work on his shoulders.

That's just how I'm going to think of this, she told herself determinedly, as work. Purposeful activity to help poor Adam relax.

Staunchly, she laid a cream-slicked hand on either side of his powerful neck. He gave a low, satisfied groan as she began to knead the hard knots of muscle that moved out to his shoulders.

Slowly, deeply, she rubbed, pummeled and punched at each of his shoulders and out to his arms. She kept her concentration on easing the muscles beneath her hands, and was pleased to feel them gradually relaxing. As she worked over him, his big body perceptibly loosened beneath her soothing touch.

After she'd pulled and stroked his hands right down to his fingers, she worked her way back up to his shoulders and began slow, deep long strokes on either side of his backbone.

He sighed contentedly beneath her hands.

Lorna smiled, realizing that the knot in her throat had disappeared. Somehow, by putting her attention on the action of the massage, it had become an end in itself. She'd stopped thinking of what might happen between them *if*. There was only his smooth skin and the muscles beneath.

Lorna closed her eyes, reveling in the feel of him under her hands. She took her thumbs and set them by the nubby bones of his spine, rubbing in an outward circle, working her way down until she had to lift her hips from the saddle of his buttocks to go farther.

Then she realized that perhaps she'd gone far enough. Gently, she lowered her hips to his again and lightly slid her hands back up to a less dangerous location.

"You continue to amaze me, Lorna Smith."

His voice, when he'd said nothing for so long a time, surprised her slightly. The tone of it surprised her even more. She'd never heard him sound like that. Lazy, content...*relaxed*. A soft smile curved her lips. However mixed her motives might have been, she'd succeeded in her objective. Under her soothing hands, Adam Gantry had managed to loosen up a little.

She put her hands on his shoulders again and bent her head down to his. "Feel better, don't you?"

"Much." His warm breath stirred her hair, which had fallen across his face when she leaned down to him.

Not questioning her action, only feeling *close* to him at that moment, intimate with him in the way she'd never really been with any man, she pulled her head back enough that the fall of hair stroked across his cheek and down his neck.

He groaned softly, and she thought he breathed her name as she went on teasing him with the cascade of tumbled curls. His muscles, which she'd worked so hard to relax, tightened again beneath her. But it was a good kind of tightness, a luxuriant awakening of desire and physical need.

Lorna forgot all about her resolve not to ravish the man. She felt herself, suddenly, as a flame of pure feminine sensation, her only desire to feed the fire of her man's need.

And Adam Gantry was definitely her man. Now, tonight, in all his masculine strength and beauty, he was everything the old, inhibited Lorna might have dreamed of in her most secret fantasies. And for the new Lorna, he was power and steadiness and the promise of wild fulfillment beneath a steely mask of self-control.

She put her lips where her hair had been. His skin was smooth and scented faintly of her lotion. She kissed him, first with just her soft lips, feeling him, learning him. And then she opened her mouth and tasted the firm skin with her tongue.

"Lorna." He said her name again, almost pleadingly.

She went on kissing him.

"Lorna . . ." His body moved, beneath her hips.

In an instinctive answer to the call of flesh to flesh, she began to stroke herself against him, in a rhythm as old as time.

And she went on kissing him, sliding her lips and tongue upward until she found his neck, and his mouth that kept murmuring her name.

He strained his head to meet her hungry kiss and when their lips met, as she lay almost full-length against him, he deftly turned over beneath her, catching her as she slid off him, and settling her back on top of him, but this time front-to-front.

His powerful arms, freed now to have their own way, wrapped around her, and then slid over her shoulders until his hands cupped and held her face. He lifted his head, hungry for her as she was for him, and he kissed her, deep and aggressively, his fingers thrust deep in the bronze spill of her hair.

Unashamed, Lorna opened her mouth to him. His sweet tongue learned all the secret, moist places beyond her eager lips.

The kiss went on and on forever, and as their tongues sparred and stroked and teased, Lorna let herself be aware of all the places she was touching him. At that moment, touching him seemed the most important thing in the world.

She sat atop him, her knees on either side of his waist, and her stomach and chest against his, with only the barrier of her T-shirt between them. Below her gently rocking hips, she could feel the hardness of him, the readiness, and everything that was woman in her responded with a sensation of opening, of sultry invitation.

He'd kicked the blanket down, so as her hands made questing forays across his skin, she felt the elastic band of his briefs and realized he was wearing nothing else.

As he playfully bit her lower lip, and then licked it, she decided she wanted to be closer to him. Closer even than she was while half lying on top of him.

She wanted to be rid of the barrier of her T-shirt, to feel her soft, full breasts against his hard chest. With a last nipping kiss that promised much, she placed her palms on his shoulders and levered herself to a full sitting position astride him. He groaned, luxuriously, as her hips made even closer contact with his.

She looked down at him, at his hard body and his handsome, squarish face and his green eyes that were now luminous with wanting, with sensual need.

Very slowly, she crossed her hands in front of her and grasped the hem of her shirt. She pulled it up and over her head, losing the hold of his shimmering gaze for only seconds.

She felt the cool air on her bare skin, as she dropped the shirt beside her on the tousled red spread. Naked but for a wisp of silk on her hips, she captured his gaze again.

He was shaking his head. The shimmer was still in his eyes, but dampened a little.

"Uh-uh," he said. He gazed on her bare breasts, and she saw the fire leap again in his eyes, just as she saw him quell it. "We need to stop this now."

She began to register just exactly what was happening. She was as nearly nude as it was possible to be, straddling Astrid Gantry's son in an ugly motel room in Winslow, Arizona.

He felt around near her thigh, and came up with her discarded shirt. Numbly, still reorienting herself to the reality of the situation, she clutched it against her chest.

With stunning sensitivity, he stroked a strand of hair behind her ear. "You are beautiful," he said gruffly. "And I'd like nothing better than to let nature take its course."

"But?"

"I don't think I'm ready to be another notch on your garter belt."

The lump was back in her throat. "Oh, I see." Slowly, she slid off of him to the worn carpet at the far side of his bed. Turned away from him, she pulled the shirt over her head and felt it mercifully drop around her thighs, covering her flushed nakedness from his sight.

She slid him an over-the-shoulder glance, since he was so deathly silent behind her. Caught off guard, his gaze burned into hers, smoldering with the heat of unsatisfied desire. He instantly averted his eyes.

"Give me just a minute," he growled. Then he was off the bed and headed for the bathroom. She didn't miss the way he scooped up his car keys again before leaving her alone.

He needn't have bothered, she thought with as much irony as she could muster in her state of frozen embarrassment. At the moment, she was too stunned by her own actions and by his rejection of her, to move. She stood rooted to the spot until he returned and slipped again beneath the covers of his bed.

"Lorna."

She refused to answer him, but realized she couldn't stand there staring at the far wall forever. She began to edge around the foot of his bed back to her side of the room. Never in her life had she felt so empty and deflated, so utterly alone and undesirable. Even Jeffrey's leaving her hadn't made her feel this bad. Some siren she'd turned out to be.

"Lorna, come back here."

She marched resolutely to her own empty bed. And she almost made it. But then, six-foot-one of nearly naked male stopped her by grabbing her arm.

"Please let me go."

"Not until you look at me." He pulled on her arm.

She slumped to the bed beside him. His hand, as usual, felt good—warm and secure. She squeezed it, her sense of humor slyly beginning to poke its head through the heavy veil of her mortification.

Then she turned her head slightly and dared to meet his steady look. He was sitting up against the headboard again, the spread once more tucked around his waist. He grinned, crookedly, and she felt her own lips curving upward in response.

"So much for helping you relax," she said wryly.

"The massage did help." He looked completely sincere.

"May I go back to my own bed now? My feet are freezing."

He tipped his head to the side, considering, and she was reminded of Astrid. And then he was sliding down under the covers, guiding her by the shoulders to stretch out beside him, with the blankets between them.

"I like the way you feel against me," he said simply in her ear. "It'll help me relax if you sleep here."

"You mean it will help you relax if I can't even move without you knowing it."

"Um. Whatever." He wrapped an arm around her waist and tucked her closer against him. His big, solid body felt wonderful wrapped around her back.

"But my feet are still freezing," she gave out, sounding sulkier than she meant to, like a child who hadn't got her way and now hungered for pampering to make up for being thwarted.

Adam reached up and flicked the wall switch, turning off her lamp and his simultaneously. Then he flipped the chenille spread off of himself and over her, keeping the blankets and sheet underneath for himself. He carefully tucked the spread around her and then gathered her close again. "Better?"

"As a matter of fact, yes." She pressed her feet against the warmth he was generating from under the blankets and felt marvelously cozy.

"Now go to sleep," he instructed softly in her ear.

But that was easier said than done.

Outside, some late-night customer slammed a car door and shortly thereafter a trunk lid. A diesel truck rumbled by on the street. From the bathroom, she could hear the steady dripping of that leaky faucet in the sink. The drip, to her ears, seemed to make a chiding noise. It sounded like her conscience, clicking its tongue in disapproval at her multiplying deceptions.

Lorna was feeling guilty again for misleading the poor man whose warmth and strong arms felt so good around her. He was a good man, a *real* man, one who cared for those he loved and always put right behavior above his own fleeting desires.

And he *had* wanted her. Now that her first humiliation had faded, she could see that clearly. But he'd felt it wouldn't be right to make love with her, given who he thought she was, and given the short time they had known each other. So he'd called a halt—later than he should have, perhaps, but at least before it was *too* late.

Now, with the heat of his body dispelling the pre-dawn chill, she felt so *close* to him. And it was a closeness far deeper than the warmth their bodies shared in the darkness. She felt just as close, though in a totally different way, as she had felt when she'd thrown wisdom to the winds and started making love to him.

But, no matter how close she felt to him, in a few hours, she was going to be called upon to deceive him again. And that made her feel as guilty as a naughty child.

She wished, fervently, that she didn't have to do it. But she couldn't let Astrid down, not now when she'd given her word to meet the older woman alone.

However, her conscience scolded, *there's also the matter of your real identity. Nothing's stopping you from telling him that. You could manage to explain it without betraying Astrid at all, if you tried.*

But then he won't look at me like I'm the most wild and wonderful creature in the world anymore....

Real closeness always begins with honesty, her con-science reminded her.

Tucked against Adam's broad chest, Lorna sighed. And then she spoke.

"Adam? There's something I haven't told you. Something I want you to know...."

She let her voice trail off and waited for his ques-tioning response.

None came.

"Adam?"

His chest moved in and out, even and slow against her back.

Lorna squirmed under his arm enough to roll face-up, so she could see him. He made a protesting noise and snuggled up closer to her, tucking his head into the curve of her shoulder.

He was sound asleep.

Lorna smiled, and allowed herself to trace the bridge of his nose with her index finger. "Never mind," she whispered. "We can talk about it some other time."

Still smiling, she rolled to her side again and settled cozily back into the curve of Adam's body. Then she closed her eyes.

Lorna woke to the insistent beeping of her travel alarm. She instinctively reached out toward the sound, before it occurred to her sleep-drugged mind that the clock was way over on the far side of the other bed. Groaning, she struggled out of the masculine arms that held her and scrambled across the other bed, managing to silence the irritating sound at last.

In the resounding quiet that followed, she sank to a crouch on the empty bed, clutching the alarm between her hands. She stared at the face of the clock for a time, then she slithered off the far side of the bed and peeked through the drapes.

It was still dark. The blinding motel sign out front went on blinking Vacancy. Lorna dropped the edge of the curtain and sat down on the bed again, putting the alarm back on the nightstand.

Finally actually waking up, she looked over her shoulder at the man on the other bed. He was snoring very softly.

"Adam?" she tried.

He went on snoring. Lorna thought it a nice kind of sound, even and soft, like a big cat purring with contentment. She longed to crawl back in beside him and let him purr in her ear until at least noon.

But there was her promise to Astrid to think of. If Adam was really as sound asleep as he seemed, now would be the time to get out of here. She could find some way to while away the time until seven, though what specifically, she wasn't sure.

She glanced out the window again. Besides looking dark, it all looked quiet as a tomb. Not a soul in sight. She'd be lucky to find somewhere to wait until the Boca Grande Café opened at, she assumed, some time before seven.

Lorna straightened her shoulders and ordered herself into action. As stealthily as she could, she darted about the room, tugging on a pair of trim jeans and a white embroidered shirt from her suitcase, giving the ordinary clothes dash and flare by pairing them with her new white boots and fringed jacket.

Then she scribbled a brief note and propped it up with the keys he had guarded so carefully, right on his nightstand, where he would see it first thing should he wake before she returned. Adam was still snoring happily when she tiptoed out the door.

* * *

As the door clicked shut, Adam opened his eyes. The enchanting little witch had made good her escape, just as he'd intended.

Tossing back the tangle of blankets, he jumped out of bed and began rapidly pulling on his clothes. As he buttoned his cuffs, he quickly scanned the note on the nightstand.

Starving for donuts. Be back soon.

L.

"Donuts, hah!" he muttered, as he slid on his shoes and reached for his jacket.

Her leaving the keys told him much. Chances were she was meeting his mother, and that the meeting was going to take place somewhere nearby.

All he had to do was keep up with her, and he'd get to the bottom of this whole mess at last. He felt rejuvenated; he'd actually slept for over an hour with Lorna's delectable body tucked up against his own. It had been a deep, satisfying kind of sleep, too. The type of sleep he rarely experienced. So that the length of it had mattered little; it had renewed him. He felt ready to tackle anything: even his mother and her tempting little bronze-haired secret sister.

He pocketed both his car keys and the room key and let himself out the door. He strode purposefully past the silent row of rooms and the darkened office until he reached the street. There he hesitated, sticking his head around the side of the building to peer down both sides of the street.

Lorna Smith was nowhere in sight. In the time it had taken him to pull on his clothes, she'd ducked into a side street, evading him though she didn't even know he was on her tail.

Her temporary escape didn't faze him in the least. She couldn't have gone that far on foot anyway. He'd methodically cover all the nearby streets on foot himself, until he found her, and then he'd hang back until he discovered exactly what she was up to.

Caught up in the chase, Adam didn't stop to analyze the smile that played on his lips or the lightness of his step as he stalked Winslow's predawn streets. Adam Gantry hadn't allowed himself enough fun in his life to recognize when he was having it.

Lorna briskly strolled the few blocks to the café and learned that it would open at six. She had a little over half an hour to kill.

She spent the time walking, aimlessly exploring the quiet streets of the desert town as the sun pinkened the expanse of sky in the east. At last it was six o'clock and she returned to the café.

The solitary waitress poured her coffee—and left her alone. Lorna watched the waitress for a while as the tall, thin woman flirted with the only customer at the counter, a man who wore his cigarettes rolled up in the sleeve of his white T-shirt and had a tattoo on his bulging bicep that said THELMA FOREVER. So much for forever, Lorna thought wryly, remembering that the waitress's name tag had said VONDA RAE.

There was an old-fashioned jukebox selector on her table, so Lorna thumbed through it. She chose a few love songs which she played in honor of Vonda Rae and her new love, Thelma's ex. In the middle of a K. T. Oslin song, Vonda Rae returned with the coffee-pot.

Just then the pay phone on the wall rang. Vonda sauntered over to it.

"Boca Grande. Just a minute, I'll check." She put her hand over the mouthpiece and held it out toward Lorna. "You Lorna Smith?"

Lorna nodded and took the phone. Vonda Rae went back to flirt with Thelma's ex.

"Did you manage to get away from Adam?" Astrid asked without preamble.

"He's sleeping like a baby back at the motel."

"Wonderful."

"Astrid, what is going on? Adam says you ran out on your own engagement party. He says your fiancé has locked himself in his room and won't come out."

Astrid made a disbelieving noise in her throat. "Maxwell will be fine. I wouldn't be in love with him if he weren't a survivor."

"Then you *are* in love with him?"

Astrid sighed. "Totally and completely, I'm afraid."

"Then *why* did you run out on him?"

There was a silence on the line then Astrid said, "Marriage is a big step for me. I've never been married. I must be absolutely sure."

"But what are you *doing*?"

There was no answer. Astrid, her voice suddenly sly, asked a question of her own. "Tell me, what do you think of my son?"

Lorna groaned. "He's an overbearing stuffed shirt who wants to control everything and everyone in sight."

"He's perfect for you," Astrid declared smugly. "I've thought it over, and I've decided that you two are meant for each other."

Lorna made her voice slow and patience. "Astrid, the makeover was great, but this is going too far."

"Tell me you're not attracted to Adam."

"Astrid—"

"Just say it, and I'll drop the whole plan."

"What plan?"

"You *are* attracted."

Lorna didn't speak for a moment. Unbidden images of the night before had risen in her unruly imagination. She saw herself sitting on Adam Gantry, felt his hands in her hair and his lips against her own....

"All right, Astrid. I'm attracted."

"Ha. I knew it."

"But it's all one big mess. He thinks I'm some wild and free mantrap on the make who's out to keep you from being happy with your fiancé and maybe steal your hairdressing salon besides. He thinks our support group is an anticommitment cult."

"I'm sure you'll work it out eventually. In the meantime, are you having a great vacation, or what?"

"Astrid, you're not listening."

"Darlin', I have a few more old boyfriends to look up in the next couple of days."

"But *why*?"

"I told you. I have to be sure."

"Adam said you kissed some guy right in front of his wife in their frozen yogurt franchise in Palm Springs."

"That was Artie," Astrid's voice went musing. "Such a sweetheart. And I know I loved him, once. But when I kissed him, all I felt was longing—for Maxwell."

"You're traveling around the country, kissing your old boyfriends?"

"More or less. I've got to be sure. If the flame still burns with any of them, then I'll have to tell Max I'm simply not the marrying kind."

"But where are you going?"

"Back to where I started, eventually. Hot Springs, Arkansas, where I was born and raised. Meet you there in, say, six days. Saturday, the twentieth. Just don't tell Adam until then where I'm going."

"Astrid, you're asking the impossible."

The sultry voice dripped reproach. "Well, I suppose you'll do what you have to do."

"I'll have to keep lying to him."

"Not lying exactly. Just not revealing all the truth."

"Astrid, it's wrong."

"Do you know he's never had a vacation that I can remember? He was a driven little boy and he's a driven man. When he was ten, he got his first paper route. He was working at a fast-food franchise as soon as he was legally old enough. He held down two jobs while he put himself through UCLA. For relaxation, he has a fitness trainer who comes to his house and tortures him with push-ups and sit-ups until he's so exhausted he can finally sleep a few hours—did I mention he's insomniac?''

"You didn't have to. I found that out myself."

"Darlin', this is all unfolding just as it should."

"Astrid, I hate it when you go mystical on me."

"Admit it. When you drew my name as your secret sister, you thought, 'What in the world will I ever have in common with a woman like that?'"

"There's nothing to admit. We both know that's how I felt. You felt that way about me."

"But we were wrong. We were meant to be sisters, so I could follow you to Palm Springs and realize at the same time that I must reexamine my own engagement. I have to do what I'm doing so I'll know if Max is right for me, and you lost Jeffrey because it is your destiny to discover other dimensions to yourself. It all fits together because Adam followed me, and as you discover your other selves you will also aid my son in learning that there's more to life than work and rigid self-control. Isn't it marvelous?"

"It's a mess," Lorna reiterated.

"It's life," Astrid declared. "And it's mad and marvelous!"

At that moment, Lorna spotted the blond-haired man who was pushing through the glass doors at the other end of the café.

"Uh-oh," she said.

Seven

"What is it?" Astrid asked in her ear.

"Adam. He's found me."

"Then I must go. Meet you at noon Saturday in front of the main post office, Reserve Avenue at Central in Hot Springs." And then Astrid hung up.

Looking resignedly grim, Adam strode toward her. He took the receiver from her hands. He held it to his ear, heard the silence on the other end, and very gently put it back in its cradle.

Then he took her by the arm. "Where are you sitting?" He sounded very reasonable.

She pointed at her coffee cup and he guided her back to the table. He signaled to Vonda Rae, who tore herself away from her boyfriend long enough to take Adam's order. Lorna didn't even object when he presumed to order eggs, toast, bacon and hash browns for her as well as for himself.

"I was feeling pretty cheerful," he said after Vonda Rae had placed a large tomato juice on the table and left them alone. "Until I walked in here and saw you were already on the phone." He sipped from his juice. "That was Astrid, wasn't it?"

Lorna nodded. "You weren't asleep at all," she accused.

"Not after your alarm went off. But I lost you, getting dressed. I passed this place once already, but it was closed."

"I went for a walk until it opened."

He eyed her warily from across the table, silently sipping again and again from his glass. Lorna knew he was trying to devise a new approach, trying to come up with a way to pry Astrid's whereabouts from her.

Vonda Rae appeared, slid their breakfasts in front of them, and then strolled away again.

Lorna discovered she was hungry. She spread jam on her toast and mixed her eggs with her hash browns and dug into the hearty fare.

While she ate, she watched Adam, just as he was watching her. He watched her like a duelist, looking for an opening. She, on the other hand, was studying him.

He'd been in such a hurry to follow her, that he'd left his tie behind. The top button of his shirt was undone, his collar flying. His hair was still mussed from sleep. Lorna thought he looked wonderful, a bit rumpled and windblown. Comparing him now with the image of tense perfection he'd presented yesterday in the hotel hallway, she decided she much preferred him delightfully mussed.

Made uneasy by her steady regard, Adam smoothed his hair back with his fingers. "What are you staring at?"

She swallowed a bite of toast and tried to keep from grinning. "You forgot your tie."

"I was in a hurry." He sounded deliciously defensive.

Naughty Lorna took over. "You should forget your tie more often. You look like a rumpled bed. It's very sexy."

He gulped down the bite of egg he was chewing and pointed his fork at her. "I want you to behave yourself."

She looked at him from under her lashes. "Do you, Adam? Do you *really* want that from me?" She shook her head. "I don't think so." He glared at her. She tipped her head, still studying him, and then she heard herself say,

"Adam, the . . . situation's been reevaluated. It's been decided that you're welcome to come along with me if you want to."

He was looking at her through narrowed eyes. "Reevaluated? By whom?"

"Who doesn't matter." Lorna could hardly believe she was doing this. But, the more she thought about Astrid's convoluted reasoning, the more that reasoning made sense. Adam Gantry needed a crash course in lightening up. Lorna Smith was making progress with him. In six more days, she just knew she could work wonders. He'd come so far already.

"Lorna, this is insane. Come along with you *where*?" he was demanding.

She let the silence stretch out before answering. "On my vacation, of course."

"Tell me the truth."

"I can only say that it'll all be over within a week."

"A week?" He uttered the word as if she'd asked for a lifetime. "I can't afford a week. I have clients who depend on me, responsibilities that I can't possibly put off."

She knew the grin on her face was a cunning one. "You mean maybe Max would have to stop sulking in his room and go back to work if you don't go home?"

"Maxwell Hollander is not sulking. He's devastated."

"So, he could use a little extra work to make him forget his personal problems."

"You have absolutely no comprehension of Maxwell's feelings or my professional circumstances, Lorna. I'll thank you to refrain from making light of them."

She popped the final piece of bacon in her mouth, and pushed her plate away, sighing airily. "Of course it's up to you. I certainly can't force you to come with me."

"Just tell me here and now where I can find Astrid."

"But, Adam, I have no idea." And it was true. At least until Saturday.

He ran his hand again through his adorably mussed hair. "I'm tired, Lorna, very tired."

"I know. Because you never sleep." She looked up from under her lashes. "But you slept with me, didn't you? If I hadn't been foolish enough to set that alarm, you'd still be sleeping."

"I'm not talking about *that* kind of tired," he insisted.

"But what other kind of tired is there?"

"There are a hundred other kinds of tired." His voice, usually so low and controlled, was getting louder. "Tired of being led across the country by two loony women. Tired of being made a fool of. Tired of being *lied* to. Tired of being totally and completely in the dark as to what the hell is going on!" He was on his feet, pounding his fist on the table, before he caught himself. "I have had it, Lorna! Up to here!"

From the counter, Vonda Rae stared. Her boyfriend applauded.

"That's tellin' her, man!" The boyfriend cheered.

"Earl, you hush up," hissed Vonda Rae.

Adam glanced over his shoulder at Earl, who stuck a hammy fist in the air in a gesture of encouragement.

"Thank you," Adam said gravely.

Earl nodded and lit up a cigarette.

Adam sat down. He pushed his half-finished breakfast away. "My appetite has disappeared."

Lorna wanted to reach across the table and touch him—a soothing touch. But she held herself back, because she knew the last thing he wanted right then was to be touched by her.

After he'd been staring morosely at his congealing eggs for several seconds, Lorna realized some kind of action was called for. She stood up.

Immediately, his gaze pinned her. "Where are you going?"

She tossed some money on the table, including a generous tip for Vonda Rae. "Back to the motel." She restrained herself from asking if he was coming, betting that he wasn't ready to let his only clue to Astrid escape, no matter how fed up he was with the situation.

Adam watched her go. Then he asked the waitress for more tomato juice and carried the glass over to the phone on the wall.

He reached Manny McGill at home, still in bed. Manny and Adam had attended high school together. Adam had used Manny's detective agency more than once in the process of preparing a case.

"Anything you can come up with, Manny," he said after he'd given him the information from the business card as well as Lorna's home address. "This one's personal, and I need it soon. I'll call you. Tomorrow, or as soon as I get the chance."

"I'll do what I can," Manny promised.

Lorna was sitting beneath the tasseled swag lamp at the little round table in the corner, poring over her map, when she heard Adam's key in the lock.

He closed the door quietly and came up behind her.

"Where are we going next?" he asked. He didn't sound too happy, but the words were the ones she'd been longing to hear.

Relief—and excitement—flooded through her. She didn't bother to restrain herself anymore. She jumped up and threw her arms around him. "Oh, Adam. We're going to have such a good time. Just you wait and see."

Reflexively, his arms went around her and he hugged her in return, but only for a moment. Then his hands were at her waist, setting her back so he could look at her. "You really do behave as if this is nothing more than a crazy, impromptu vacation." He was eyeing her with obvious suspicion.

"But that's exactly what it is," she answered, utterly ingenuous.

He grunted in disbelief and dropped his hands from her waist. Then he snared up his tie and went to the vanity mirror to put it on. "I'm going to need to stop and buy a few things." He watched her watching him in the mirror as he efficiently looped and knotted the tie. "This shirt is a disgrace and my suit needs cleaning. And here at the Super Duper Motel, they've never heard of a concierge."

"Mr. Impeccable," she mused fondly.

"What did you say?" He was brushing his hair with a brush from the little emergency overnight case he'd brought in from his car.

"Er, I said that's do-able."

"Do we still have to be in New Mexico by noon?"

Quickly, Lorna calculated. The distance chart on the map said they were a little over a thousand miles from their Saturday destination, if they were to take Highway 40 straight through. But, of course, she planned on several detours. Random detours. Into delightfully off-the-beaten-path locations.

"Plans have changed. We need to be near Albuquerque by evening," she improvised.

"Plans are always changing," he muttered dryly. "As if you were making them up as you go along."

"You've found me out," she replied with mock remorse. Then she bent over the map spread out on the table. They were two hundred and fifty miles from Albuquerque. They had plenty of time to reach there by evening, and enjoy the sights along the way.

Done making himself as impeccable as possible under the circumstances, Adam said, "I'll call my office from the car. Let's go."

Adam drove in silence as they left Winslow behind. To her few attempts at conversation, he grunted or gave terse answers. Lorna quickly decided she wasn't going to let him get away with this for the whole drive. Her assignment, as both she and Astrid saw it, was to get him to lighten up. So she soon began casting about for ways to accomplish her objective.

At Holbrook, when they'd been on the road for about half an hour, Lorna had him pull off at a roadside dairy stand. Adam declined to follow her inside, apparently reasoning that she wouldn't be ditching him in the middle of the desert when she could have so easily escaped him in Winslow.

She bought two Fudgie Bars—a decadent concoction of vanilla ice cream, fudge syrup and fudge topping speckled with nuts, all stuck on a stick and guaranteed to elevate the blood sugar and expand the waistline. Remaining obstinately cheerful, she bounced back out to the car, slid into her seat and held one out for Adam, who was already turning the key in the ignition.

"What is *that*?" He looked at the ice cream bar as if she planned to poison him with it.

"Fudgie Bar." She bit into hers, sighing voluptuously.

"No, thank you," he said, as she continued to hold his out for him. He started to shift the car into reverse.

"Suit yourself." She shrugged, and laid his bar, still wrapped, on the little pull-out cup holder beneath the dashboard.

"It'll melt there," he said.

"I'll take care of it in a minute," she said between slurps.

Lorna realized with an internal smirk of satisfaction that he seemed momentarily to have forgotten all about what a hurry he was in to get back on the road where he could go on driving he knew not where in ominous silence. Instead, he watched her with a kind of grim fascination as she continued nibbling at the nutty semisweet fudge crust that encased the layer of snow-white ice cream, and the thick ooze of more fudge beneath that.

"It's not even nine in the morning." The words were disapproving, but the tone was mesmerized.

"But it's so *good*." With her tongue, she licked at the creamy vanilla where she'd revealed it by nibbling off the chocolate.

"But it's not good *for* you." He sounded like he was trying to convince himself, even more than her.

She looked at him, steadily, as she continued to lick the melting confection. She was thinking how sexy green eyes could be, and how the person she'd been two days ago would never have indulged in anything so debauched as a Fudgie Bar.

"Adam." She stroked her tongue up the stick, where a dribble of vanilla had almost escaped. "Life is all about balance."

He blinked, then tried to assume a superior air, though the huskiness of his voice betrayed him a little. "What do *you* know about balance?"

"I'm learning. Every day." She picked up his Fudgie Bar again and waved it tantalizingly at him. "Have you ever even eaten a Fudgie Bar?"

"No, and I never will." He didn't sound terribly convincing.

"How sad for you. You're missing one of the premiere experiences of life." She took her attention from her own bar and peeled back the wrapper on his very delicately, with her teeth.

He shook his head, slowly, like a man spellbound by a sinuous snake. "I'm not going to eat that."

Her lips curled upward and she leaned across the console toward him. "Say that like you mean it."

He looked down at her, and the hunger in his eyes had nothing to do with a craving for ice cream. "I'm not going to kiss you, either," he said, the words seeming to drop from his lips of their own volition.

"Um. Just like you weren't going to kiss me back in the parking garage in Palm Springs."

"That thing is melting."

"Then lick it."

He did. "You have to start learning to consider the consequences of your actions," he said as soon as the ice cream no longer endangered his slacks.

"Oh, but I have. I am. Come on, Adam. Another bite." He did as instructed, while she polished off the last of her own bar. "Your mother tells me you're obsessed with physical fitness," she said as she continued to feed him.

"My mother's entitled to her opinion." The engine was still running, so he fumbled for the power window switch.

"What are you doing?" she asked.

He took her stick and the remains of his ice cream bar and tossed them neatly out his open window into a waste can by the car door. "There," he said, turning back to her. "That takes care of that."

"Oh, well," she gave in gracefully and began pulling back to her side of the car. "At least I got you to take a little taste."

"Wait." He held on to her elbow.

"What?"

"You've got chocolate..." He took his handkerchief from his pocket and dabbed at the corner of her lip. "There."

Lord, she wanted to stretch just the little distance it would take for her lips to meet his. But in the moment it had taken him to dispose of the sweet treats, she'd decided she wasn't going to throw herself at the poor man again. He'd begin to think her insatiable. For this magical week, she might be wild and free. But she was stopping short of insatiable or heaven knew what might transpire.

Adam seemed to have forgotten that there was no need to keep holding on to her arm, now that he'd so considerately dabbed the bit of chocolate from her mouth.

"Thank you," she said and tugged lightly, to remind him that he could let her go now.

He held on, gently. She could have broken his grasp if she'd wanted.

But she didn't. "Adam—"

"I'm not going to kiss you," he said, each word slow, husky, and deliberate.

"I think you told me that already."

"We're going to be in close proximity for a week."

"That's right."

"Boundaries have to be set. Limits maintained."

She tried a little smile. "Okay. No more Fudgie Bars, I promise."

"I'm not talking about ice cream."

"Fine. I get the message. You can let go of my arm now."

He held on, and spoke firmly. "I want you to stop teasing me. I don't want to take advantage of you." His expression softened. "I have a feeling you've been taken advantage of too much in your life."

"Don't bet on it," she said, without thinking.

"Go ahead." His voice was tender. "Treat your pain as if it's all a joke. But I know you've been hurt, Lorna. And hurt badly. No woman lives on the run like you are without a reason."

"Well, now," she said. "I won't argue with that."

With the hand that wasn't holding her arm, he smoothed her wild hair back away from her face. Lorna felt her breath stick in her throat. He'd done the very same thing the night before when she'd been sitting on top of him, nude to the waist.

"So beautiful, and so confused," he said, his voice soft as melting ice cream. "I want to help you, Lorna. If you'll let me."

It occurred to Lorna that she'd very much like to be helped by him. Especially if he'd go on stroking her hair in that tender, wonderful way. "Adam, I think..." But her voice trailed off as she realized she had no idea at all what she thought.

"Were you mistreated as a child?" he prompted.

She shook her head, and told the truth. "My father sells insurance and my mother's a teacher. I have two sisters, one older, one younger. Both prettier and more popular than I ever was."

He blinked, as if she'd surprised him. "Two sisters," he mused. "Is that so?"

"Yes. We lived in Long Beach, California."

"I see." His tone made her suspicious, though she couldn't quite put her finger on why. It was as if he were correlating information, though how he could do that when he had no information but what she'd given him was beyond her. "Tell me more," he coaxed.

Shrugging off her suspicions, she continued, "My parents still live there. I have a degree in library science from Cal State Long Beach. And I own a bookstore, in Westwood."

His eyes gleamed, briefly. "A bookstore. In Westwood."

"It's the truth," she said, feeling noble.

"I'm sure." The words were bland.

"Is there anything else you'd like to know?" she asked in saccharine tones after a moment.

He didn't miss a beat. "Tell me about the *support group.*"

"I told you. It's a group of women who get together every week to share—"

He cut her off. "How did you become involved in it?"

"There was an ad. In the *L.A. Weekly.* I felt there was something missing in my life, a closeness with other women that I'd never found with my mother or my sisters. My mother's kind of undemonstrative, you see. And I never had much in common with my sisters. We weren't close at all. They were both so outgoing and gorgeous. But I was the bookworm—the mousy one."

"The mousy one." He repeated her description softly.

Lorna sighed. "You don't believe a word of this, do you?" He just went on looking at her, measuringly, not even stroking her hair any longer. "I suppose it would fit in better with your idea of me if I said my mother ran a bordello in New Orleans and I went to work there myself at a very tender age. Or if I told you

I'm the runaway daughter of one of the Beverly Hills One Hundred, spoiled and indulged until I have no other purpose in my life but where to find the next good time.''

"Is that closer to the truth?''

She pulled away from him, then, sharply. "I've told you the truth," she said, staring out the window at the redwood fence that separated the dairy-stand lot from a gas station.

"I guess I just can't see it through all the lies," he said.

Sitting back in her own seat, she turned to him. "By the end of this, you'll know everything. I promise."

"Do you have convincing evidence as to why I should believe your promises?"

Lorna shrugged. "You might as well believe me as not, since you've decided to go with me either way."

"The logic in that argument escapes me completely."

"Because it's not logical. It's just good sense. Why brood and pout all the way across the country, when you could just as well relax and have a good time?"

"I never pout. Is that where we're going? Across the country?"

"Right now let's take that road there." She pointed. "It leads to the Petrified Forest National Park. Or so the sign on the highway said."

Without another word, Adam shifted into reverse and backed out of the dairy stand onto the road she'd indicated. Lorna turned on the radio and punched the digital channel selector, looking for a program to fill the testy silence between herself and Adam. She found a country station that kept fading in and out, but still the wavering signal was better than listening to nothing and feeling the emanating disapproval from the driver's side of the car.

In twenty minutes, they reached the park. Lorna turned off the radio then and exclaimed over the brilliantly colored remains of ancient coniferous trees. Adam grunted occasionally and piloted the car with a kind of dogged determination that cast a dreary pall on all her efforts to have a good time. He followed her through the Rainbow Forest Museum with his hands in his pockets, not saying a word. He refused to even let out one "ooh" or the slightest "ah" over Agate Bridge, a huge petrified log that spanned a forty foot ravine. And though he accompanied her to Newspaper Rock on a 120-step trail down the face of a cliff, he glared at the Indian petroglyphs there as if they, too, were keeping secrets they had no right to conceal.

Lorna tuned back into her country and western station when they merged back onto the main highway at a little past noon.

"Go on straight through to Gallup," she instructed Adam blithely. It was becoming like a contest between them. He refused to crack a smile; she absolutely would not relinquish her good humor. "We can stop and buy you the things you need there." She tossed him a broad, friendly smile. "If that's okay with you, of course."

"Wonderful," he said flatly.

Lorna began tapping rhythm to the music on her blue-jeaned thigh, and humming along. She stared out the window at the big, pale sky and the occasional cotton-puff clouds and the red desert that seemed to go on beyond forever, broken only by scrub-brushed hills and high mesas. The flat tablelands fascinated her, thrusting as they did straight up from the desert floor, their sheer sides almost purple where they were shadowed from the bright midday glare.

Adam stopped for gas just before they crossed the New Mexico state line and they reached Gallup before two o'clock. They ate mouthwatering chili at a place called the Ranch Kitchen where the waitresses wore bright gathered skirts and Lorna exclaimed over the beauty of the authentic Navaho rugs hanging on the walls. Adam ate in silence, giving her little more than a nod and a grunt now and then.

He chose an ordinary department store in which to buy his clothes, but Lorna did find it gratifying when he emerged from the dressing room. He was wearing tan jeans, boots and a plaid shirt and carrying several more shirts and jeans in various colors.

"Don't give me that smug look," he muttered, as he added a sheepskin jacket to his pile of new clothes. "If you're going to be dragging me up and down cliff faces to stare at Indian rock paintings, a business suit is totally inappropriate."

"I couldn't agree with you more," she said, knowing full well that she sounded every bit as smug as she looked. Even though he was still scowling, he had to be considerably more comfortable in the casual clothes—and comfortable was good. Comfortable was a plus in the direction of lightening up.

The sales clerk agreeably hung and bagged Adam's much-abused suit. "Tonight," Adam told her as he paid for his new vacation wardrobe, "we stay at a decent hotel where I can get this suit cleaned and pressed."

Some adventure, Lorna thought wryly. Driving around with a stuffed shirt whose major concern is getting his suit cleaned.

They were returning through the store to the car, laden with purchases, when she spotted the sleeping bags on sale in the sporting goods section.

She stopped and set down the bags she was carrying. "Adam, I see something we need."

He followed the direction of her gaze. "No," he said. "Oh, no."

"Oh, Adam. I've always wanted to camp out."

"You said Albuquerque tonight," he accused darkly. "There are plenty of good hotels in Albuquerque."

"I said *near* Albuquerque."

"So? There's no problem. You can go where you have to go and do whatever you have to do and then we can find decent lodgings and get a good night's sleep on actual beds."

"You know you won't sleep anyway," she chided. "So what does it matter whether you don't sleep in some boring hotel room or out beneath a blanket of stars?"

"This is rattlesnake country," he threatened. "And at night it gets cold up in the mountains around Albuquerque. Snakes are attracted to warm, close places. Like a sleeping bag."

"How do you know?" she quizzed suspiciously.

"Astrid's my mother, remember? When I was a kid, she dragged me all over this country. She went through a back-to-nature phase when I was not quite in my teens. We slept out under a *blanket of stars*," he stressed the words ironically, "enough times to last me the rest of my life."

"Good," Lorna enthused. "Then that means you're an expert. We won't have any problems."

"Lorna, why do you always insist on taking what I tell you and twisting it to fit your next harebrained scheme?"

"We have to sleep out, Adam," she told him solemnly.

"Why?"

"Because I'm receiving my next set of instructions sort of out in the middle of nowhere. In the middle of the night."

"*Sort of* out in the middle of nowhere? Where exactly is that?"

"You know I can't tell you," she said. She thought, mainly because I don't know yet.... "Now, watch these bags, will you?"

"Lorna..."

"Be right back."

Eight

"The weather report said a forty percent chance of rain."

"Adam, don't be such a pessimist. There's not a cloud in sight."

"Desert storms can strike almost without warning."

"We're not in the desert anymore, or didn't you notice?"

"In spite of the occasional piñon pine, this is still semiarid territory. Storms can come and go in a flash."

"Fine. When it starts to rain, we'll get in the car."

"Do you realize how far we drove on unpaved road to get here? We'll be driving back through a quagmire if it rains. My car is hardly an all-terrain vehicle."

"So, it'll be a challenge getting back. Now, I don't want to hear one more word about the weather. Please?"

"Don't ever say I didn't warn you."

"Never. I'll never say that."

"And beyond the threat of thundershowers, this whole escapade has no logic to it whatsoever."

"How so, Adam?"

"Do you actually expect me to believe that someone's meeting you out here in the middle of nowhere?"

"Believe what you like. I'm waiting for. . . a message."

To that, the man on the sleeping bag across the camp fire gave a disbelieving grunt and fell blessedly silent for a time.

Lorna, lying on top of her sleeping bag but under a blanket from the car, sighed in gratitude for the moment of peace and laced her hands behind her head. She stared up at the stars that seemed like holes of light in the black fabric of the sky.

They were camped up against a large rock near the base of a brush-dotted mountain at the end of a nameless road somewhere northwest of Albuquerque. Their fire had burned low between their bedrolls and now Lorna felt the heat from the coals as a lovely warmth on one side of her face.

The fire, like just about any other subject one might care to name, had been a bone of contention between them.

"We don't have a permit," Adam had argued.

"But we haven't seen a soul for miles. We probably don't even *need* a permit," Lorna reasoned back.

"This is the end of the twentieth century, Lorna. You need a fire permit almost everywhere now. And where do you think we're going to get the wood any-way?''

"There was that dead tree by the road aways back."

"You want me to go back there and throw it in the trunk on top of your designer luggage?"

She'd refused to be drawn. "I'll be glad to help you."

So, against Adam's better judgment, they'd had a fire. She'd admired his expertise in building it, using the pieces of wood they gathered from the fallen pine and a few broken-up tumbleweeds for kindling.

"At least the wood isn't wet," he had grumbled when the logs caught and the blaze was crackling away.

As night crept across the mountains and the thin air acquired a bite that soon became a true chill, they'd eaten sandwiches bought before they left the main highway and shared a thermos of steaming tea.

"What kind of message?" Adam prodded from the other sleeping bag, putting an end to Lorna's musing on the hours just past.

Lorna shifted her position a little to avoid a few rocks that were poking her in the back. "Isn't it beautiful out here?"

"What I'm asking is, are we expecting someone?" Adam pressed on.

"Expect . . . the unexpected," Lorna advised.

Adam, who'd been stretched out on top of his sleeping bag, now sat up and wrapped his arms around his knees. Aware of his movements, Lorna rolled to her side, propping her head up on her hand and grin-ning at him across the red coals of their fire.

"Come on," she said. "This isn't so awful, is it?"

He utterly surprised her by giving her that charming smile that had been so depressingly absent through most of the day. "No, it isn't so awful," he confessed. He tipped his head, thinking.

"You know, I can see Astrid in you when you do that." The words were out before she considered if the mention of his mother would snap him back into surly silence.

But he took no offense. "When I do what?"

"Tip your head like that. Even if you'd never told me your name, I would have figured out you were related eventually because of the similarity when you make that gesture."

"But you knew me the minute I said my name."

"Yes."

"Because Astrid had told you all about me, right?"

"Yes."

"In your *support* group, I suppose."

"Yes. In our *support* group."

"What did she say?"

"Adam, I can't tell you that. What gets said in the group has to be completely confidential, otherwise no one would speak freely."

"I see."

Of course he didn't see. Not at all. And Lorna knew that was mostly her own fault. She looked away for a moment, off to the southeast and the slight glow on the horizon that must be the lights of Albuquerque. When she looked back at him, he was staring into the fire, a funny half smile on his face.

"When I was ten, Astrid took me on my first camping trip."

"Where to?" she prompted softly, pleased by his change to a reflective mood.

"Near L.A. In the Los Padres Forest. It was just as her beatnik phase was coming to an end."

"Astrid had a beatnik phase?" Lorna could hardly picture the bright, bubbly Astrid as having had a beatnik phase.

"You name a phase," Adam said, "and Astrid's had it."

For a moment he said no more, so Lorna asked, "What was it like—your first camping trip?"

"A nightmare."

"Oh, Adam. It couldn't have been that bad."

"No?" He looked up from his contemplation of the fire long enough to meet her eyes. "Do you really want me to tell you what it was like?"

She nodded. "In detail."

"Why?"

"Oh, honestly, Adam. I like you and I like your mother. I'm always interested to learn about people I like."

He granted her another dubious glance, but then he gazed into the red embers of the fire again and began to speak.

"I remember the two of us driving to the edge of the Dick Smith Wilderness. Night was coming. The sky was orange and purple to the west. At twilight, Astrid parked the car by the side of the road and handed me my roll of blankets while she tucked her own up under her arm."

Adam chuckled wryly. "Those blankets were straight off the beds at our apartment," he explained. "I, at least, was wearing tennis shoes and jeans. My mother had on a black minidress, black heels and black tights. You see, she'd decided to go camping more or less on the spur of the moment, as she did just about everything."

One of the logs, burned through, collapsed in the red bed of coals, sending sparks arcing in the air between them. A section of smoldering log rolled beyond the ring of coals. Adam took the stick he'd been using as a poker and pushed it back in among the glowing embers.

"As I said, it was already almost dark by the time we parked the car," he went on. "And she just marched right out into the bushes on the edge of a dry wash. I followed. She walked for over an hour in high heels, her dress and tights getting torn to shreds, but she didn't even mind. She was singing the whole way. Bob Dylan songs. 'Blowin' in the Wind' and 'One Too Many Mornings.' When she finally got too tired to take another step, she just stopped and laid out her blankets on the rocky ground. I stood there beside her. I was so *angry* at her."

"For dragging you out there like that out of nowhere?" Lorna asked.

He grunted. "For that, yes. And for a thousand other reasons. For being different than other guys' moms, for never having meals at regular times, for falling in love with a new man every other day, for creating an aura of excitement around herself where I could never relax from one minute to the next because I was always wondering, *what next?* Where will she drag me off to, what will she say that will embarrass me in front of my friends?—not that I had many friends. We were always moving, always going someplace better that never turned out to be any different than the place before—'' He caught himself up short, and his eyes, which had been focused on the past, fixed again on Lorna's face across the fire. ''Anyway, when she stopped and laid her blankets on the ground, I was mad.''

''And then?''

''She looked at me. And she knew I was furious. She gave this little half shrug and she said, 'Adam, I wish I could be the kind of mother you want. But what I am is the only mother you've got. I'm doing my best, baby. But I'm looking for something. And until I find it, things are always going to be just a little bit up in the air in the Gantry household.' ''

''So you came to an understanding?'' Lorna asked quietly.

''Not at all,'' Adam said. ''I was still furious. But, as the years went by, I did realize that she always did her best for me. It wasn't easy, especially in those days, for a woman to raise a child on her own. But I was one responsibility that she never tried to shirk.'' He laughed again, dryly. ''Until I was old enough to be on my own, whatever trouble she got into, she took me right along. And yet she never tried to hold on to me, either. I was allowed to stay home alone from sixteen on. And as soon as I turned eighteen, I moved out on my own with her blessing.''

"So the point is," Lorna concluded, "that even if Astrid wasn't exactly the mother you might have chosen, she was an excellent one on the whole."

"The point is," Adam amended with an irritatingly superior glance, "that I never forgot what she said on that camping trip. A month ago, when she told me she was going to marry Maxwell, she showed me her ring and she smiled at me in that mysterious little way she does at times—you know the way I mean?"

"I do," Lorna said.

"She said, 'Baby, I think I've found it at last.' And she meant it, Lorna. I know she did. After years of searching, she's found someone she could be happy with for the rest of her life." He stared at Lorna challengingly across the remains of their fire. "And now she's throwing it away."

Lorna gazed back at him, that dangerous ache of tenderness moving within her again. Tenderness mixed with the familiar longing to give him the truth. It would ease his concern for Astrid if he knew she was only making sure that her marriage to Maxwell was the right step. And if he knew the truth about Lorna herself, well, he'd drop her off in Albuquerque in the morning and return to his well-ordered, well-pressed life.

"I suppose—" she sat up and wrapped the blanket around her against the increasing chill in the air "—that this whole thing with me just reminds you unpleasantly of when you were a little boy. Being dragged all over the place without really knowing why."

"It has occurred to me that there are certain similarities," Adam replied.

"How old are you, Adam?"

"Thirty-six." He narrowed his eyes at her suspiciously. "Why?"

"And for the first sixteen years of your life you were at the mercy of Astrid's urge to find herself."

"Yes, that's about right. What are you getting at?"

"That leaves the last twenty years where you've done exactly what you want when you wanted. Where you've had nothing but order and predictability."

"I wouldn't go that far," he cut in, too quickly. "Life is never entirely predictable."

"But in so much as you could make it that way, it *has* been for you?"

"I don't like the direction of this conversation."

"Because you know my conclusion already."

"Then there's no need for you to draw it." He was giving her that jade-eyed glare, hard and impenetrable as rock.

"Balance, Adam," she drawled amiably, once again feeling justified in keeping her secrets for a while longer. "Life is all about balance. And you've been too long in too much control."

For his part, Adam was finding the tenor of this discussion increasingly uncomfortable. "No one can be in too much control of his life." He loathed the defensive tone of his own voice.

"He can if he finds it's turned dry as dust in his hands." Lorna was talking about her own life as much as Adam's.

But Adam had no way of knowing that, and now, with that remark, he realized she'd hit something inside him that recoiled at being touched.

My life is not dry as dust, he said firmly to himself. My life is well ordered. My life is already balanced.

But, for some absurd reason, he kept seeing his closet at home with his rows of shining shoes, arranged by color and wearability on wooden shoe trees—business and dress shoes in front, casual wear behind. He saw the rows of hangers with his suits on them, every hanger hooked over the bar front to back. His shirts were all folded precisely, and his sweaters the same.

"You're so perfect, Adam," a woman he'd dated seriously had told him the year before. *"Too perfect. And completely self-contained. You're a wonderful lover, so I must admit I'll miss that part of our relationship. But, still, there's always been a part of yourself that you've held back. If there's ever going to be someone to break through your reserve, it's not me or I would have succeeded by now. . . ."*

Adam shut out the memory of his ex-lover's words and came back to the present to find himself staring at the fire-flushed face of his mother's secret sister.

Lorna was wrapped in the lap blanket from the car, her hands hugging her knees, so he could see nothing but her naughtily grinning face, the tips of her white boots and all that glorious hair. He thought of how that hair felt, trickling like liquid silk through his hands. He thought of the milky globes of her breasts the night before, when she'd tossed her shirt over her head and driven him almost insane with longing to let go of every shred of reserve and control he'd ever possessed. He'd wanted her to take him inside her, to take him to that place of total abandonment that her every sultry glance had promised since the moment they had met.

Damn you, Lorna Smith, he thought, glaring at her as she grinned back at him. Why, with all of the suitable women that there are in the world, did it have to be a footloose temptress like you who would make me want to lose control?

Lorna stared back at him, wondering what on earth was going through his mind. His glare was hard and hot, sending conflicting messages of both anger and desire. Her nerves tingled in what might have been warning or anticipation. She lost her grin as she gathered the blanket closer about her, suddenly feeling uncertain and vulnerable. Images of the night before flashed through her mind—of Adam's hands in her hair, his lips on hers, of his body so beautiful and strong beneath her as she sat astride his hips.

He'd wanted her, a lot. Only his much-vaunted self-control had kept him from having her. And he could have her any time he wanted, Lorna admitted to herself as she watched him watching her. And if he did ever decide to make love with her all the way, *then* where would she be?

The fantasy Lorna might take such intimate activities in stride. But not the real Lorna Smith. The real Lorna Smith would be bound to him, and she had a sinking feeling the bonds would be much harder to let go of than dealing with Jeffrey's desertion had been.

A shiver skittered up her spine and Lorna drew the blanket even closer about her. Maybe, she thought, she should be grateful that Adam Gantry was such a demon for self-control.

At that moment, Adam tore his gaze from hers and began pulling off his boots and shrugging out of the sheepskin jacket he'd bought during their afternoon's shopping spree.

"I take it this conversation is terminated," Lorna said, trying for lightness, though it came out a little strained.

"I'm turning in," Adam said. "Maybe you'll get lucky and I'll actually fall asleep. Then when your *message* arrives, you won't have to try to keep me from intercepting it."

Lorna decided that the wisest course would be to withhold further comment and follow his lead. She took off her boots and jacket and crawled into her sleeping bag. After a few minutes of fitful wriggling, she managed to arrange herself for a minimum of discomfort around the various pebbles and rocks that kept trying to poke her. Far off, she heard a howling sound—a wild dog or a coyote barking at the sliver of moon. After that, sleep fell upon her like a curtain of night.

In the distance, someone pounded a massive drum. The pounding was intermittent and without any discernible rhythm. In her dreams, Lorna beheld a giant Apache warrior looming over the land, resplendent in war paint and feathers, beating a tom-tom with a huge mallet.

Someone shook her and urged, "Lorna, come on. Wake up. We have to get out of the open."

Lorna grumbled and snuggled farther under the covers, trying again to get comfortable in spite of the rocks in her bed.

"Lorna, come on. It's going to rain."

As if to punctuate those words, the Apache in her dreams hit the tom-tom with all his might.

Lorna groaned, rolled to her back and opened one eye. "Whazzat?" she said.

Adam was looking down at her. "Thunder."

Lorna sat up. It was still dark. Overhead, the stars were being swallowed up as thunderclouds devoured the sky. Billowing and rolling they came, with the speed of a rushing train, obscuring the thin slice of moon until it could barely be seen. Straight bolts of lightning cracked out of the sky to the northwest, followed by the crashing of thunder that Lorna recognized from her dreams. For a moment, as the cobwebs of sleep cleared, Lorna just stared up at the sky. Then she threw her arms out, as if she could embrace all of nature's magnificence in her two slender arms.

"Oh, Adam," she cried. "Isn't it spectacular!"

"Hurry up," Adam ordered. He had his rolled sleeping bag under his arm and was headed toward the car. "We've got five minutes tops and then it'll be pouring rain." He tossed the words over his shoulder at her as he rushed to the car.

Lorna began pulling on her boots, but apparently she wasn't moving fast enough for Adam. After throwing his sleeping bag in the trunk, he charged back to her side.

"Get up."

She did as instructed, jumping on one foot to get the other boot on. With unbelievable speed, he rolled her bag and trotted to the car with it while she stuck her arms in the sleeves of her fringed jacket.

"Adam, a little rain isn't going to kill us," she called out good-naturedly, flipping her tangled hair out from under the collar of the jacket and tipping her face up to the wild, roiling sky.

At that moment, the sky cracked open and a wall of cold water fell on her face. And kept falling. Lorna couldn't believe it. It was as if there were firemen up there with a hose trained on her. She was so stunned by the suddenness and force of the deluge that for several seconds she stood and let it soak her to the skin.

Then Adam grabbed her arm. "Come on." He started running for the car and since he had a firm grip on her elbow, she was dragged right along behind him.

When he reached the vehicle, he yanked open the passenger door and shoved her in. Then he ran around and got in on the driver's side.

Lorna sat in a puddle made by her dripping hair and clothes and stared out the windshield at a wall of water punctuated fitfully by javelins of lightning. Adam started up the engine and turned on the heater.

Then he began taking off his clothes.

He dropped one boot and then the other behind his seat, followed by his tan Levi's and then his plaid shirt. His socks stayed on, apparently because the practical boots he'd bought had kept them dry. Lorna gaped at him, amazed partly at his dexterity in getting out of his clothes in the confined space and partly struck once again by the masculine perfection of his body.

"Get those clothes off," he commanded. "You're soaked to the skin." He'd apparently managed to grab a few things from the trunk, because he reached into the back seat and came up with one pair of his new blue jeans and a new shirt. He then slithered into the jeans by sliding around to face her on the seat and shoving one beautifully formed, rock-hard hairy leg and then the other down inside. He shimmied them up over his briefs and buttoned them quickly. Then he stuck his arms in the shirt, not bothering to button it. He laid an arm across the back of the seat and turned to her.

Lorna, who had pressed herself against the door to give him room to maneuver, realized she was staring at his deep, broad chest framed by his open shirt—and that the chattering sound she kept hearing was her own teeth knocking together.

"I said, get out of those things." He levered himself up, tossing the order over his shoulder as he reached in the back seat. "I got one of your suitcases from the trunk. I hope there's something warm in here," he said.

Teeth still chattering, Lorna cast a glance to the back seat, only to see a froth of lace and satin spilling out of the suitcase in question. He'd chosen the one with her honeymoon lingerie in it.

"What is this?" Adam demanded, disgusted. "A whole suitcase full of underwear?"

"Nightwear," Lorna corrected through clenched teeth. She'd discovered that clenching them kept them from knocking together.

"I'll refrain from comment," he said, shaking his head.

"Do that," she shot back. "There should be a T-shirt or two at the bottom."

He dug around and came up with one. "You can use the blanket, too." As he grasped the blanket she'd been wrapped in earlier, she silently applauded his foresight. He'd remembered to throw it in the cab while stowing her sleeping bag in the trunk.

Blanket and T-shirt in hand, Adam slid back over the seat to the front. "You're still dressed," he accused when he was facing her again. "And you're shaking like a leaf. Strip. Now."

Lorna began peeling off the ruined jacket and then the soaked white shirt. She was down to her lacy bra on top when Adam said gruffly, "Never mind the bra. There's not enough of it to worry about anyway."

He shoved the T-shirt at her, and she pulled it over her head. "Now, give me your feet," he ordered. "One at a time." Numbly, she did as instructed. He took off the soggy white boots and threw them in the back with his, likewise her thin socks. "Your feet are like ice cubes," he muttered. "But we'll deal with them in a minute. First, the pants."

She wriggled out of them, with much less grace, she thought, than he had. With the wet clothes gone and the heater blasting away, she found that her teeth no longer needed to be locked together to keep from chattering.

She giggled, softly, as he reached toward her, engulfing her in the big, warm blanket, draping it over her head for a minute and using it as a towel on her hair.

"You find this all hysterically funny, I take it," he grumbled, scrubbing at her hair with the towel.

"I was just thinking how much better you are at taking off your clothes in a confined space than I am."

"And that's funny?" His golden brows drew together. They were still wet from the rain, as was his hair. He smelled wonderful, she thought. A cool, wet smell of wood smoke and rain and man.

Lorna reached out from the cocoon of blanket. "Your eyebrows are crooked." With her fingers, very lightly, she smoothed them into even wings.

He caught his breath, and she let her hand stroke down over the chiseled planes of his face and neck to the crisp mat of damp hair on his chest. His skin was so warm and resilient beneath the corkscrews of hair, just as she remembered from the night before.

"You're still a little wet here." She let her fingers curl in the whorls of hair. Her voice had that purr in it. She didn't really know how the purr had gotten there, because she wasn't doing it on purpose.

Adam caught her hand. He held it motionless between them and his expression was very still. Very controlled. Then he released her and slowly backed to his side of the car.

Lorna realized at the same time as he did that neither of them was breathing. To the droning of the rain on the car was added the sound of a mutual indrawn breath.

"Give me your foot," he said.

"Adam, I . . ." she heard herself say. And then she couldn't go on. There were so many ways to go on. *Adam, I want you. Adam, I'm not who you think. Adam, the real me is frightened. Adam, would you... Adam, could you still want me if you knew...*

He interrupted the words she didn't have the courage to utter. "Let me rub your feet. You have to get warm, Lorna," he said with calm logic. "We can't leave here until dawn. Even though the rain will probably stop soon, those dirt roads we have to drive on are going to be a disaster. In daylight, I'll at least be able to see what's coming. And I can't leave the engine on all night. We'll run out of gas."

Hesitantly, she slid around in the seat and lifted her bare feet, swinging them into his lap. His hard thighs beneath the blue jeans were warm as toast.

"You're warm." She said it simply, with no coquetry at all.

A smile, all the more welcome to her because she knew it came unbidden, curled his mouth. "How do you do it?" he mused. He began stroking her feet with his big, strong hands, bringing the blood and the heat back into them.

"Do what?" She was thinking about how lovely it felt as he rubbed her arch and massaged each of her toes, and about how there was a rightness to it. Last night, she'd massaged him. Tonight it was his turn to do the work.

"Sometimes, it's as if you're someone else altogether," he explained.

Lorna swallowed, and almost pulled her foot away. But he held on and continued with that delicious rubbing. "Someone else?" she dared to ask.

"Yes, someone kind of shy. Someone utterly unsure of herself as a woman."

Lorna stared at him. Inside her, a war raged.

Tell him now, one part of her mind commanded.

It'll all be over if you do, another voice inside her head shot back.

His hand felt so wonderful, caressing her foot. The time they'd had together had been so short. And parts of it had been utterly magical. Only a few more days, a time apart. To be the woman she could never be in real life. But the price was continued deception; if she told the truth, most likely the next few days would be ended before they even began.

Lorna quickly shifted her gaze out the window. "Look. You were right. The rain's stopping."

He kneaded the ball of her foot, and she knew he was staring at her quizzically. She said nothing, but kept her gaze out the window. She could feel his shrug through the hands that caressed her foot as he decided not to pursue the mystery of her shier self. She tried to disguise her sigh of relief.

Outside, as quickly as it had come, the storm left them. The rolling clouds rolled on toward Albuquerque, and the sliver of moon shone its bright sideways grin once again.

"Better?" Adam asked as he left off stroking her foot.

Lorna sat up again while Adam buttoned his shirt. "Much." She wrapped the blanket down around her bare feet. "What now?"

"Adjust your seat back all the way, and then I'll turn off the engine. You can try to sleep until dawn."

Lorna pushed the little button and the seat slid to a nearly prone position. She settled herself in, and was aware that Adam, next to her, did the same.

For a time, she lay there, looking through the beads of water on the windshield at the stars and the hump-backed shadows of the mountains that surrounded them.

"Lorna?" Adam's voice in the silence startled her.

"What?"

"What about your message?"

She rolled her head to look at him, and saw in the darkness the gleam of his eyes and the upward curve of his mouth.

She grinned back at him. "It's not morning yet."

He grunted. "Shall I tell you what I think?"

"Why not?"

"I think this whole trip out here was designed to throw me off the scent."

"You do?"

"I think you'll be making a simple phone call when we get to Albuquerque tomorrow and that's where you'll find out where to go next."

Lorna turned her head and stared out the windshield again, saying nothing.

Adam assumed her silence meant he'd guessed right. "Lorna, I want you to tell me something," he said after a moment.

She turned to him again. "Adam, I can't—"

He lifted a hand. "Let me finish." It was his turn to glance away. "Look. I've thought about what you said tonight. And maybe you're right. Maybe there *is* something missing in my life. And maybe it wouldn't hurt me to follow someone else's lead for a few days."

Lorna sat very still, hardly daring to believe what she was hearing.

"There are just three points that would have to be clarified," he went on, turning back to face her at last.

"Yes?" The single word that she tried to make sound neutral came out thick with suppressed hope and excitement. Five more days, she was thinking, of Adam and me and a whole big country to explore!

"One," he said grimly. "I have to know." He pinned her with a look, his eyes boring through her, seeking the unvarnished truth. "Is there anything illegal about this group you and my mother are involved in? Any nefarious activities *whatsoever*—from tax evasion to fraud to... drug running. Whatever. I want the truth, Lorna. And if you lie, I may not know what you're holding back, but I'll be able to sense you're not being honest."

For once she was able to look him right in the eye and not worry if he'd guess all that she wasn't telling. "Nothing, Adam. Nothing illegal at all. I swear to you."

He sighed, and she realized it was a sigh of relief. "I can see you really believe that. So whatever negative activities are going on, you, at least, aren't involved in them purposely."

Lorna made a concerted effort to quell her exasperation. "Adam, I don't only *believe* it, I *know* it."

He waved his hand at her. "All right. We've been going in circles on the subject for two days now, so let's put it to rest for a while. We won't bring it up again until this *vacation*, as you insist on calling it, has come to an end. Agreed?"

"Absolutely." In her mind's eye she was picturing the magical week stretching ahead of them.

"Point number two," he said.

Lorna sat up a little straighter in the laid-back seat. "I'm listening."

"We'll be traveling companions," he explained. "You'll tell me where we're going and I'll get us there without argument. I'll even do my best to be cheerful about it—"

"Wonderful," she couldn't help interjecting.

"But," he said.

"I'm listening."

"Point number three is that we *won't* be lovers."

Lorna felt her face flaming at the directness of his demand. She was glad that the darkness hid her reaction from his sight. "You mean I have to stop trying to seduce you, is that right?"

"There are too many things you're keeping secret from me, Lorna. I could never feel right about myself if I made love with a woman I didn't even know. And it wouldn't be fair to you, either. I hope you can understand that."

"Well." Lorna cleared her throat. A part of her was grateful, because she knew that physical intimacy between them would be terribly dangerous for her. The naughty Lorna, however, was already wondering just how long he could hold to his resolve in the face of sharing every moment with her for the next several days. "Yes, all right," she said at last. "I do understand."

"Bluntly," he reiterated, "I mean no sex."

"No sex. I heard you," she said levelly. "But I want you well rested if you're going to be doing the driving."

"Don't worry, I'll be fine."

"Fine isn't good enough. You have to sleep."

"What are you getting at?" He eyed her warily.

"Turn on the engine and lever these seats out of the way." She tossed back the blanket and bounced over the headrest to the back seat. Then she began tossing all the soggy clothing to the front.

"Lorna, I asked you—"

She hoisted her suitcase of lingerie into her own empty seat. "Put the seats up," she ordered. "And get back here."

He'd turned around and was glaring at her warningly. "Lorna, we just agreed—"

"Oh, stop it. I'm not going to entice you, for heaven's sake. I'm just going to make sure you go to sleep."

"How?"

"We'll sleep together."

"What kind of a solution is that?" He looked at her as if she'd finally gone over the edge.

Disgusted, she planted her hands on her hips as she sat scrunched between the two laid-back seats. "Adam, you fell asleep with me beside you last night. I'm betting you can do it again tonight. I think you *like* sleeping with me.''

He shook his head, his eyes accusing.

''Oh, Adam. Why can't you stop thinking everything that isn't logical is immediate cause for suspicion? So you like sleeping with me next to you, so what? Don't analyze it. Just be grateful that for tonight at least you can get some rest.''

He tipped his head and she knew she was swaying him.

''Put up the seats, Adam. And get back here with me.''

He did as instructed, not saying another word.

Fifteen minutes later, as she lay against his chest listening to the steady beating of his heart and the gentle rhythm of his breathing, she found herself unable to quit thinking of the promise she'd made that they wouldn't be lovers during the days to come.

After all, it's for the best, the real Lorna reassured herself.

But the naughty Lorna wasn't nearly so resigned.

You'll be mine within twenty-four hours, the wayward temptress promised silently, laying her hand possessively over his heart.

Lorna and Adam slogged into Albuquerque at a little past noon the next day. Lorna raised not the slightest objection when Adam checked them into a high-rise luxury hotel. They shared a suite of two bedrooms and a sitting room.

He left her to luxuriate in strawberry bath salts while he found a garage to investigate the strange creaking that had been issuing from the undercarriage of his car ever since they'd hit a particularly deep mud hole on the way back to civilization. While the car was being serviced, Adam placed his call to Manny McGill.

"Sorry, Adam, no dirt," Manny announced. "What we've got here is a nice, straight lady who pays her bills before they're due. The bookstore exists and Lorna Smith owns it. She's got two sisters, three little nephews and one niece. Her parents are Mr. and Mrs. Suburban America. She *is* in a support group with your mother, but it's just that, a bunch of women kibitzing over their problems.

"The only semihot tidbit I could find is that this Lorna just got dumped by her fiancé. But she took her honeymoon anyway. In Palm Springs. Her employees expect her back in a week or so."

"Manny," Adam said, "this woman isn't the marrying kind in the first place. And if she were, you can bet *she'd* be the one to do the dumping." But even as he spoke, he was putting things together, remembering Lorna's suitcase full of honeymoon-style lingerie, her scrubbed-clean face in her driver's license photo, and, when they'd been outside the dairy stand in Arizona, she'd given him her own half-serious description of herself as "mousy."

"So," Manny suggested, "maybe you're dealing with an impostor."

"No," Adam said, thinking of Astrid's skill with makeup and a blow dryer. "I think I've got the real thing here. What I have to figure out now is what I'm going to do about it."

* * *

Lorna was all dressed for a night on the town when Adam returned before five. He told her she looked beautiful, said the car was as good as new and then he disappeared for a half an hour into the bathroom on his side of the suite.

He emerged scrubbed and shaved and, best of all, smiling. As he asked, "Where to, now?" Lorna realized he really did intend to uphold his end of the bargain. He'd go where she instructed—and without complaint.

She decided they would explore Old Town, the Spanish heart of thriving, modern Albuquerque. Adam was marvelously agreeable, so they toured the beautiful San Felipe de Neri Church and wandered the shops and galleries of Old Town Plaza. As dark drew on, they ate arroz con pollo in a lovely Mexican restaurant.

"Tired?" she asked him when they emerged from the restaurant.

He smiled at her. "No. Why?"

"I don't know. You seem kind of far away."

"Just thinking." He took her hand, with none of the wariness he usually displayed when he touched her. Enchanted as always by the pleasure just his touch brought her, she curled her fingers in his.

"I suppose you'll want to go dancing," he said.

But she didn't want to go dancing. She just wanted to be alone with him, though she knew such a wish was again tempting fate.

She said, "I don't think so. No dancing. Not tonight."

"The hotel then?"

She nodded. On the way to the car he continued to hold her hand. They drove in silence through the brightly lighted streets, sharing few words during the time Adam parked, or in the elevator, or even after they entered their suite.

The fully stocked wet bar in the sitting room included a complimentary bottle of good champagne, which was chilling in the half icebox beneath the marble counter.

Adam offered her a glass. She nodded, and watched as he expertly popped the cork and poured the fizzy beverage into a pair of crystal flutes. When he handed her her glass, she suddenly thought of Astrid, just three nights ago, proposing a toast to "the new Lorna Smith."

Adam raised his glass. "To you, Lorna Smith," he said in an eerie echo of Astrid's words. "Whoever you are."

He was smiling warmly. There was absolutely no taunt in the salute at all. Yet Lorna felt like crying.

She downed one obligatory swallow of champagne and set her glass down. "I think I'll turn in."

He arched a brow at her. "Alone?"

Lorna cleared her throat. "Well, yes, I mean..." She drew in a breath and ordered herself to stop stammering like a schoolgirl. "You're the one who asked for two bedrooms, remember?"

He waved his hand as if that had been a momentary aberration on his part. "You know I can't sleep without you. And I imagine you'll have me driving all over the country tomorrow. I need to be well rested.

For the sake of highway safety." He took a step toward her. She stared at the open collar of his shirt, and the skin of his strong neck. She was thinking how smooth his skin was. And how wonderful to touch.

"I'll help with the driving," she heard herself say.

"But I like to drive." His beautiful, sensual mouth moved softly, tauntingly.

Lorna realized she was leaning toward him. She caught herself, stepping abruptly back. "I'm going to bed, Adam," she said firmly.

He only smiled. "Sleep well, Lorna."

But sleep wouldn't come. Instead, Lorna lay in her bed and wondered what in the world had happened.

Since he'd left her to fix the car in the afternoon, Adam had been behaving strangely. He'd been so sweet and gentle, and so unbelievably agreeable, going along affably with her every whim. And he'd actually seemed to be enjoying himself. She didn't think he was pretending to have a good time at all.

Lorna shivered, though the room wasn't cold.

It was as if, without her knowing exactly when or how, the scales of their relationship had tipped. Something had happened, and now, though she was in complete control of where they went and what they did, she wasn't really in control at all.

There was just something about Adam since this afternoon. Something different. A lack of frustration. As if he were actually letting himself relax—which was just what Lorna was after, so she couldn't see why it made her so nervous.

She sat up in bed.

On edge, and not understanding why, she straightened the silk pajama top that had rucked itself up around her waist. The slinky fabric slid over her skin caressingly, and she felt edgier still.

Lorna switched on the lamp. The room the light revealed was beautifully appointed. The walls were papered in the palest yellow and ecru stripes. The furniture was rich mahogany. The bed linens, of that same ecru and yellow as the walls, enfolded her in the softest, sweetest-smelling cotton and lace. On the polished table that stood before the doors to the small balcony sat a crystal vase of fresh-cut flowers. Lorna had left the glass door open a crack and a slight breeze ruffled the filmy curtains.

It was a room to calm the senses. Yet Lorna was not soothed. She turned off the light, deciding she preferred the soft glow of the city lights beyond the gauze curtains to the brightness of the lamp.

She lay in semidarkness for a moment, and then found herself pushing back the covers and swinging one foot to the carpet.

She was spared deciding what to do next, because the door to the sitting room opened.

Lorna gulped. "Adam?"

"I've changed my mind," he said, his face in shadow, his powerful arms and shoulders outlined in the golden light beyond the open door behind him. He wore the bottoms to a pair of striped pajamas she'd watched him buy the day before.

"About what?" Her voice was low, and seemed to come from outside herself.

"Our agreement." He left the doorway and approached her, his bare feet whispering across the expanse of eggshell-white carpet.

"Oh," she murmured, inadequately. Then, not knowing what else to do, she swung her feet back beneath the covers, making room for him to sit on the edge of the bed. She waited for him to start asking questions again, to demand to know who she was and where Astrid was and what, exactly, was going on.

Lorna let her head drop backward onto the curving headboard of the graceful sleigh bed. She stared up at the shadowed ceiling. She decided that she was going to tell him everything. Get it all out in the open, just as soon as he asked.

But he said nothing. And then he reached out and she felt the sweet caress of his fingers down the slender length of her neck.

Lorna gasped, softly, and lifted her head to look at him. He held her gaze, as his fingers deftly began unbuttoning her pajama top.

It was then that she understood exactly which part of their agreement he was referring to.

She also realized that she wasn't going to do anything to endanger the magic of this moment. In the end, the truth would catch up with her. But not now, not tonight....

"Are you going to make love with me, Adam?" she heard herself asking as the buttons continued to slip from their holes.

"Yes."

Nine

Adam peeled open the front panels of her silky top and Lorna felt the night air on her bare breasts.

"Do you know how beautiful you are?" he said.

"I am?" She looked down at her breasts. They shone like alabaster in the dim light, the nipples hardening with growing arousal.

He chuckled. "You are." She glanced up, and met his eyes again. His gaze was sleepy, full of promise and sweet desire.

He bent his golden head toward her, and he kissed her, at the top swell of one breast.

Her heart, which had been beating very fast, suddenly decelerated in rhythm, as though her blood had thickened, and now flowed through her body with the slow sweetness of honey.

She took his head in her hands, guiding him, reveling in the silky feel of his hair against her palms and through her fingers. His mouth moved slowly downward and then closed on her nipple.

The honey in her veins turned molten and she groaned as he suckled her, first gently and then more insistently, until she felt she had been turned inside out by the hot, increasing demand of his mouth.

Then his lips stopped their magic torment. She clutched his golden head closer, unwilling to let him go. In answer to her sensual plea, his mouth closed on her other breast, and he gave it the same stunningly erotic attention as he had the first.

Her senses reeling in a dance of escalating delight, Lorna moaned aloud. Adam lifted his mouth again from her breast. Stroking his hair, Lorna looked down into his face. His lips were full and moist with pleasuring her.

"You like that," he said, his voice like rough velvet.

"I love it," she purred with total frankness, her hands trailing down to caress his shoulders. Never in her life had she felt this free, this able to respond just as her body and heart commanded. And it was all because she was someone completely different. A magical, new self who was utterly at ease with her own sensuality, a woman who knew how to give and receive pleasure without hesitation or guilt.

Sighing, the pleasure like a voluptuous heaviness swelling every nerve, Lorna let her hands drift down his muscled arms to rest on the yellow coverlet. Then she slid to a prone position among the pillows, arching her back like a cat seeking strokes. "Kiss me there again, Adam," she said.

He chuckled. "You're greedy."

"Yes. I'm greedy for you."

He shifted beside her, lifting his weight enough that he could toss away the pile of sheets and blankets. Boldly staring into his eyes, Lorna toyed with her own hair as it spread and coiled in wayward tendrils on the pillows that cradled her head.

"Please kiss me there again, Adam," she coaxed.

"I will. Soon."

"Promise?"

"I swear it. But first..." The way his voice trailed off insinuated much.

Lorna reveled in such insinuations. "Yes. Name it, Adam. Whatever you want."

His glance licked along the entire length of her, from her fanned hair to her bare toes. "Those pajamas are very pretty."

"But?"

"But the top's covering your arms and shoulders...."

"And?"

"The bottom's covering your legs."

Brazenly, she lifted her hips off the bed. "Then take them off of me."

His white teeth flashed as he put both hands on her waist, just above the elastic waistband of the silky pajama bottoms. Lorna gasped, loving the warmth and firmness of his palms against her bare skin.

His thumbs slid beneath the elastic, and then his hands were under there. She lifted herself to help him as the silk whispered down her legs and off the ends of her pointed toes.

"Better?" she asked.

"Much." He was looking at her legs, his gaze caressing them as surely as if he were actually touching her. The skin of her thighs prickled in a wholly hedonistic sensation.

"Now, the top," he said.

Obligingly, she sat up again. He took the collar of the shirt in either hand, and began peeling it back from her shoulders. But he had to get close to do that, his face near hers, his breath warm against her neck.

Brushing her hair out of his way, Lorna turned her head toward him. What happened next stunned her with its beauty.

A kiss. Just a meeting of the lips, but a meeting so achingly sweet that Lorna wondered if she'd ever know its likeness again.

He breathed her name against her mouth, she took the breath inside herself. He went on nibbling at her, kissing her, sharing his breath with her as he guided the nightshirt down her arms, and dropped it on the floor.

Then he drew her close, deepening the kiss, and rubbing himself against her in a thoroughly delightful way, so that the crisp hairs on his chest chafed her soft breasts in a delectable torment.

She dropped her head back, breaking the lovely kiss, but losing nothing when his mouth immediately found her neck, the delicate perfection of her collarbone and at last her full breasts once more. She moaned and offered herself up to his lips, writhing with pleasure in his arms.

Soon, her roving hands discovered the elastic that held up his pajama bottoms. With little wordless, hungry urgings, losing the feel of his mouth on her breasts but intent on claiming new ground, she coaxed him to his knees on the bed beside her.

In the shadowed room, there was the sound of a woman's and a man's husky laughter, as she worked his pajamas down over his hard hips and consigned them to the floor next to her own. He had nothing on beneath.

Lorna looked down at him, thinking that every single part of him was just about as perfect as could be.

He was chuckling again. "What?"

She looked into his slumberous eyes. "Everything. You're perfect." She touched him. It was a totally natural thing to do. "All of you." Her hand closed around him.

Adam groaned, and threw his head back, muttering a short oath under his breath.

Lorna went on exploring him. "You like that?" she asked.

He didn't answer. He didn't have to. By the way he moved to her touch, he was telling her that he was hers to command.

"Adam?"

He growled in his throat in reply.

"Remember the motel room, in Winslow?"

He growled again.

"Remember how I was on top? Do you think we could do that again?"

For a moment, she stopped touching him to look into his face. He took advantage of the moment to carry her backward on top of him, giving her an answer without saying a word. And then he was sliding the little triangle of silk that covered her hips down over her bottom and off to the floor.

She reached for him again, but he stopped her. His eyes had that absolutely still, deep look that she remembered so well from the night before in the mountains, when he had taken her hands in the rain-pelted car and stopped her from touching him.

Only now, everything was changed. He *was* stopping her from touching him—but only because he wanted to touch her.

Which he did. Holding her gaze, he caressed her as she sat astride him, doing to her just what she'd been doing to him. She twisted and bucked above him, lost in the sensual glory of what he did to her, finally throwing her head back and giving in completely to the magic of pure sensation.

Beyond the filmy curtains, the city of Albuquerque glittered like a cache of jewels in a desperado's pocket. But inside the darkened room, there was only a woman and a man.

When at last he felt her complete openness to him, he guided her above him. She sank down upon him, taking him fully into her, and the sound he made at their joining was an echo of hers.

She rose up as he moved wildly beneath her, and she followed the rhythm he set. And he said things—crazy things—into her mouth when she claimed him with a kiss, and into her hair which fell in wild tangles onto his heaving chest.

Wild, it was. For both of them. An emancipation each had sought a lifetime to find. And now, locked in the most ancient dance of all, they approached freedom. The dance had a thousand different cadences. It melted and changed without prelude, so that, at last, neither knew who led and who followed.

While at first she rode him, the time came when he rose up above her and drove into her, hard and fast. And she took every inch of him, crying out rashly for more, holding him to her as his heart beat, reckless and untamed, against her breasts.

The culmination, though, came on a slow build, as they rolled to face each other. There, the rhythm established itself, like slow-rolling thunder, tumbling down from high mountains over a thirsty, waiting land.

Lorna couldn't stop crying his name, over and over, as her release came to her. She clung to him then, tightly, wondering inchoately how she had ever survived without Adam Gantry's arms to hold her and his touch to set her free.

At last, they lay against each other, heart to heart. And Lorna smiled into the darkness. Adam's breath was slow and even. He was fast asleep.

From then on, they didn't bother with the pretense of separate bedrooms. They would hang out the Do Not Disturb sign wherever they stayed and then immediately proceed to set each other free. Then later, when their passions were thoroughly spent, Lorna would sleep curled against him.

More than once, just before dawn bleached the sky, she would wake, warm in the heat of his body.

This, she would think, is what happiness is. This is love, and thank heaven I've found it at last.

And then she would remember the thousand ways she had deceived him, and long only to have the truth revealed once and for all.

"Adam?" she would whisper, hesitant but determined.

"Go back to sleep." And he would settle her more comfortably against his heart, pressing his lips in the tangled cloud of her hair.

Coward, her conscience would scold. But his arms felt so sheltering around her, and nothing was so wonderful as the feel of his breath against her hair. So she'd surrender to the moment, snuggling closer to him, closing her eyes against the coming dawn.

And then somehow, with daylight, adventure would beckon in the form of the long, leading strip of the highway. They'd snatch a quick breakfast and be on their way.

On Tuesday, just outside of Amarillo, she made Adam stop the car on the shoulder of the highway and then she dragged him across a huge grain field. In the distance, several cows bovinely observed their progress.

Adam argued the whole way that they were probably trespassing, but he too stood in awe when they finally reached their destination: ten upended Cadillacs half-buried nose-down in the rich ploughed-up earth.

Later, they would learn that the nose-down machines were millionaire Stanley Marsh III's pop-art homage to the fifties. But right then, to Lorna, the magical absurdity of the half-submerged cars charmed her utterly. She wasn't sure exactly why. She supposed it was partly the twenty rear wheels hanging in the air, as if the row of old luxury cars had dived from the sky in tandem only to land nose-down in the mud. But mostly, the sight made her think of Astrid, who had set her off on this grand adventure, and whose own Caddy had bit the dust in the desert between Palm Springs and Prescott.

"Oh, Adam, isn't it great?" Lorna breathed reverently.

Adam shook his head. "Only in America," he said. And then he pulled her into his arms, told her she was crazy and kissed her right there for all the cows to see.

"Why, Adam," she said with a sigh when he was finished. "What's happened to you?"

He gazed down at her ruefully. "Something wonderful," he said. "Something absolutely wild."

They spent that night in Amarillo. The next morning, Lorna placed another of her mysterious phone calls and then informed Adam that they were detouring down into Texas.

Wednesday and Thursday, they rode through wide open spaces and wandered the streets of Lubbock and Abilene, cutting across the center of the state to Dallas–Fort Worth and then back up through Wichita Falls. They spent the night there Thursday.

And it was as she lay against Adam in the wee hours, experiencing those nagging pangs of guilt, that it suddenly struck her: six days was a very short time. Though it seemed as if they'd barely begun, their time together was coming to an end.

After a leisurely brunch the next morning, they crossed the Red River and entered Oklahoma, reaching Oklahoma city late Friday afternoon.

"Let's just keep driving," Lorna suggested, her voice sounding too light, almost brittle to her ears. Since the night before, when she had at last admitted that the moment of truth was approaching, she'd had to make a concentrated effort to keep from bursting into tears every time she looked at the map and realized how close they were getting to Hot Springs, Arkansas.

Adam cast her a quick sideways glance, and a warm smile. "Where to?" His window was down, his dark gold hair blown slightly by the wind. He looked tan and relaxed. Fit as ever, but not one bit tense. If her goal had been to get him to lighten up, then she could give herself a big hand for a job well done.

For some reason, though, she didn't feel much like clapping.

"Lorna?" Adam's glance this time was tinged with the beginnings of concern. "Something wrong?"

"No. No, nothing." She looked down rather blindly at the map, and forced her eyes to focus on their route. "Henryetta," she said.

"Who?"

"Oklahoma. Henryetta, Oklahoma. That's where we have to be tonight."

"I've learned never to ask why." Adam smiled at her again, an open, good-humored smile, the kind of smile he had for her all the time since their magic night in Albuquerque. The kind of smile she'd probably never see again after they met up with Astrid and the full truth was revealed.

Our last night, she thought. Tonight.

Suddenly, this moment and every moment of the too-brief hours ahead seemed infinitely precious. Lorna wanted to memorize every second, to imprint each fleeting heartbeat of time on her senses for all the years to come.

She turned to look out her open window. Oklahoma farmlands rolled by, great expanses of new corn and still-green wheat. The air that swirled in to tease her hair and caress her face held the moisture of a land crisscrossed with rivers, so much different than the thin, dry air of the southwestern deserts that they'd left behind when they reached the Texas panhandle three days before.

"Beautiful, isn't it?" Adam said, sensing her appreciation.

"I wish it would never end," she said.

Adam said nothing. Lorna dared a sideways glance at him, but the glance told her nothing. He drove with easy concentration, one elbow resting in the open window.

"But it is going to end," she added, though she knew she shouldn't.

He glanced at her, and then took his gaze back to the road. "Did you imagine it wouldn't?"

"I didn't let myself think about it."

"I know."

She felt irritated with him, though she knew it was unfair. "What's happened to you, anyway?" she heard herself demanding waspishly. "You're certainly taking this all in stride."

"Isn't that what you wanted?" His tone was infuriatingly mild.

"You could at least pretend that you're going to miss me when it's over," she said, sounding like a petulant child and hating herself for it.

"Don't be a brat, Lorna. And stop trying to pick a fight."

"I'm not—"

He glanced at her again, and that was all it took. She admitted to herself that she *was* indeed being a brat and subsided into silence in her seat.

After a time, she said, "We're going out tonight, Adam."

He chuckled. "For a wild night on the town in Henryetta, Oklahoma?"

"Exactly. I'm getting a major message in Henryetta's hottest night spot."

"I see." He sounded very tolerant. Very patient. And why shouldn't he? He'd waited almost a week, and now the truth he'd bargained for would finally be his. He could wait a little longer with ease and grace.

A frantic recklessness assailed her. "It's going to be our last night together, Adam."

"Oh, is it?"

"Yes. And I'm going to do my very best to make sure that you never forget it."

* * *

The night spot that Lorna chose was only a few miles from their motel. She'd found it by asking their waitress at Ken's Pizza about Henryetta nightlife when Adam had gone to the rest room.

"You mean like a club?" the waitress had quizzed in that soft friendly twang of the native Oklahoman.

When Lorna had assured her that a club was exactly what she meant, the waitress had given her directions.

The Clubhouse, as the sign out front proclaimed, was surrounded by a parking lot bursting with cars. The building itself looked like nothing so much as a huge gray barn, complete with rounded roof and clapboard walls.

"This isn't bad at all," Adam murmured after paying the cover charge and leading her to one of the tables against the wall. Lorna said nothing in response to that, but his implication didn't escape her. Since he'd known her mood was rash, he'd probably expected some sort of honky-tonk dive.

He glanced approvingly at the two burly uniformed security guards near the door. Lorna knew what he was thinking: if there was going to be trouble in Henryetta, Oklahoma tonight, it wasn't likely to happen at The Clubhouse.

A cocktail waitress came by and Adam looked at Lorna. She shrugged. "A beer." He asked for one, too. The cool, long-necked bottles came and Lorna and Adam sat just sipping for a while, listening to the fiddle player in the band at the end of the dance floor. Lorna took in the layout of the place, thinking without much enthusiasm of how she was going to have to lose him for a while to receive her latest—and final—"message."

The big room was arranged in a horseshoe shape, with the bar at the toe end, the dance floor in the center, and the band in the heel. She and Adam sat on one side of the "shoe." Across the way were rows of pool tables.

Though she tried to concentrate on her surroundings, Lorna's gaze kept returning to Adam. He was wearing the dressy Western clothes she'd made him buy when she'd dragged him through Luskey's Western Store in Fort Worth. His yoked dress shirt had mother-of-pearl snaps. His smooth weave cowboy hat bore a Mansfield Cutter crease. A silly lump formed in her throat as she thought of the two of them, poring over the hats together, arguing over styles and colors. In the end, he'd bought the hat she liked.

He caught her looking at him.

"Love that hat," she got out over the noise from the band.

He took it off and set it on her hair, winking at her when she had to tip her head up to see him.

The wink almost did her in. It took all the will she possessed not to burst into tears. She realized she had to escape him for a few minutes, to get her emotions back in line.

She slid out of her chair, setting his hat on the table as she went. "Be right back."

"Lorna?" he asked, his voice tinged with apprehension. But she kept moving, leaving the elevated seating area behind and losing herself among the couples on the dance floor.

Not looking back, she ploughed through the dancers, murmuring "excuse me's" right and left as she went.

Lorna emerged from the dance floor and rushed up the few steps to the other side of the room, her eyes brimming with the tears she was determined not to shed. The tears, unfortunately, blurred her vision. That was why she rammed right into two hundred and fifty pounds of pool player just bending over to drop his winning shot.

Unaware of the sudden deathly silence in the immediate vicinity, Lorna tossed off another "excuse me" and tried to forge on. But the pool player grabbed her arm.

"Just a minute there, little lady," he said.

Lorna furiously blinked back the tears and stared up into a narrowed pair of small ice-blue eyes. "I—I'm sorry," she stammered. "I wasn't paying attention."

"You just blew my game." The big man's breath was ninety proof. Lorna realized that though he spoke with deadly clarity, the man was far from sober. He pointed to the felt. "You see that ball there, little lady?"

"You mean the eight ball?"

"That's right." He chose each word very carefully, as if he was talking to someone of minimal IQ. "I was just about to drop that ball, and now, see that man over there?" He pointed to a rangy character across the table, who was leaning against his cue stick and grinning.

Lorna nodded.

"That's Lester. And now Lester is going to get a turn. Lester ain't as good as me, but he's good enough."

"Look, I am really sorry—"

"Let her go." Adam's calm, quiet voice seemed to cut through the air behind her.

The big pool player was looking over her head. "This yours?" he asked, as if Lorna were something that had dropped out of Adam's pocket. "She's real nice to look at, but she needs to learn to pay attention to where she's going."

"I said, let her go."

Lorna whipped her head around to see Adam moving in. His face was utterly, terrifyingly composed. Frantically, she scanned the room for the security guards. One was across the room near the door and looking in the wrong direction. The other was nowhere in sight.

Adam had reached her side. She was sandwiched between the two men. Though the band played on and the dancers on the floor two-stepped merrily along, everyone in the immediate vicinity seemed to be watching with bated breath.

The pool player and Adam stared at each other. Lorna glanced from one hard face to the other.

"Look," she said. "I was in the wrong. Isn't there some friendly way we could settle this?"

The pool player peered down at her. And then back up at Adam. Then his broad face split in a challenging grin.

"Sure," he said. "Let's dance."

"Forget it," Adam said. "Let go of her arm."

"No," Lorna cut in quickly. "Adam, it's all right." She shook off the pool player, who released her since she'd agreed to his terms.

Placatingly, she laid a hand on the front placket of Adam's shirt. "It's okay." She stared up into his expressionless face, willing him to let her handle this herself.

After a moment, he backed away. She felt the collective exhaled breath as everyone nearby realized a fight wasn't in the offing after all.

"All right," she said to the pool player. "Let's dance." She walked ahead of him out to the floor, thinking it wouldn't be so bad to stand a foot away from him and gyrate to the music the way most of the other dancers were doing.

Unfortunately, a slow number started up the minute they reached the floor. Lorna was immediately hauled against a barrel chest by a pair of beefy arms.

"By the way, I'm Del Dearborn."

She craned her neck to look up at his heavy face—the action was also an attempt to keep a reasonable space between his body and hers.

"You mean Del as in Delbert?" she asked sweetly.

His wiry brows furrowed. "I'll let it pass this time, pretty lady, for you. But I'm warning you now. Nobody—but *nobody* calls this old boy Delbert." He yanked her close again and exhaled the threat against her ear. She was once again reminded that he wasn't entirely sober. "What's a gorgeous thing like you doing with a weekend cowboy like that?"

Lorna had the urge to stick two fingers in Delbert's beady little eyes and stomp on his arches. Instead, she murmured sweetly, "He's not what you think at all. Actually, I'm his prisoner."

"His *what*?" Delbert blessedly pulled back for a moment, long enough to scowl down at her disbelievingly.

"I'm his prisoner. He's on the trail of Astrid Gantry. And I'm his only lead."

"Who's Astrid Gantry?"

Lorna scoffed. "You never heard of Astrid Gantry?"

"Sure, I heard of him," Delbert muttered defensively. "I got a TV, you know." He yanked Lorna back against his chest. "But I don't believe you for a second, little lady. You're just havin' you some fun at this old boy's expense."

His huge hand was rubbing her back through her thin camisole top. Lorna tried to bear with that, but when his hands slipped to the pocket stitching on her skin-tight black jeans, she drawled, "One inch lower, and you'll be shooting pool one-handed, Del."

Mercifully, his hand roamed back to where it belonged. "How 'bout you and me, we ditch that guy you came with and have us some fun?" he whispered suggestively in her ear.

The dance ended. "No, thanks," she said. She whirled neatly out of his arms—and into Adam's, who had been waiting on the edge of the floor.

They danced in silence for a while and Lorna clung to him, aware from the stiffness of his body that he wasn't entirely happy with her, but grateful for his clean scent and the firm strength in his arms.

Once or twice she tipped her head to glance up at his face, appealingly, she hoped. But beneath the shadow of his hat brim his expression remained stoic. She was just about to suggest that they depart The Clubhouse and return to the motel when a beefy hand tapped Adam on the shoulder.

Del Dearborn had not surrendered the field. "Mind if I cut in?" he said, in a pushy mockery of courtliness.

"Yes," was all Adam said. He went on dancing.

"I asked real polite-like." Del's hand closed over Adam's shoulder.

"I suggest you remove your hand," Adam said. He'd stopped dancing, and so had most of the couples nearby.

"Where you from?" sneered the pool player. "Yale? And where'd you get this fancy hat?" He whipped the hat that Lorna loved off of Adam's gold head.

"Delbert!" Lorna cried, unable to contain herself. "You give that back!"

"What'd you call me?" Delbert turned on Lorna.

"Stay out of it, Lorna," Adam ordered.

"I will not. He's a bully. And he's not going to get away with it!"

"I warned you not to call me that, little lady." The music played on, but most of the dancers were still.

Lorna planted her hands on her hips. "Delbert," she said, "Give that hat back this minute!"

"Better do it, Del," one of the unmoving dancers advised. "That lady sounds serious."

Delbert dropped the hat on the floor and stomped on it.

Lorna saw red. With an exclamation of total frustration, she leaped at the big pool player. She never made it, though, because Adam stepped in front of her and neatly decked the giant with a hook to the jaw.

The rest was total confusion. When Delbert dropped among the dancers, he didn't go down alone. He was like a massive tree falling in a forest, taking everything in his way down with him. Suddenly, in the tight press, everybody had a punch to throw. All the men jumped to the defense of their ladies and everyone thought the next guy was out to get him.

It was a brawl, pure and simple. A free-for-all that the two security guards could no more quell immediately than Noah could stop the flood. As fists flew and bodies reeled around her, Lorna had only one thought: the hat that they'd chosen together. That precious hat that he'd bought to please her. Adam wasn't going to lose his hat!

She kept her eyes on it, through the milling press of bodies, as boots and high heels unheedingly kicked and pummeled it toward the edge of the dance floor.

Adam had a hold of her arm. "Damn it, Lorna, let's get out of here...." He was trying to pull her in the wrong direction.

She shrugged him off and dived for the hat. Her hand closed around the brim as Adam caught her again, yanked her up just before an alligator boot came down on her arm, and hauled her backward through the throng.

Ducking flying chairs and dodging wild punches, he dragged her behind him up to the raised level by the bar and into the hall beneath the sign that said Rest Rooms. She dared one last glance at the room as they left it. Delbert Dearborn, sporting a bloody nose and the beginnings of a black eye, was being held firmly between the two burly guards. Gratifyingly, he looked as if he'd had enough of picking fights for the night.

Adam tugged her right past the rest rooms to the end of the hall and the emergency exit there. He shoved at the red bar, cursing under his breath when the alarm went off.

Together, they ran into the cool, moist night air, pounding through the rows of cars to the waiting Chrysler. Adam unlocked her door, shoved her inside and leaped the hood to his side.

She reached across and had his door open for him before he got there. He started up the engine and backed out.

Miraculously, Adam got them out of the parking lot without incident. Lorna held her breath the whole time, because the other drivers who'd somehow also managed to escape the fracas were zipping out of spaces with no awareness of what might be behind them. To Lorna, for that heart-stopping few minutes, the parking lot seemed like a giant game of bumper cars played for real.

But soon they were back on the short strip of highway that led to their motel, and shortly after that, the

Chrysler was sliding into the parking space near their room.

The car seemed eerily silent when Adam turned off the engine.

"We're lucky we weren't invited to spend the night in the local jail," Adam said after a moment.

"I know." Lorna looked down at the cowboy hat, still clutched in her hands. It was smashed flat and covered with dirty boot prints. The unwelcome tears rose in her throat again, pushing for release.

"I suppose you're going to tell me you received your next set of instructions during the scuffle," Adam suggested blandly.

She forced herself to look at him, feeling the tears pooling in her eyes and willing them not to well over and disgrace her completely.

"No, Adam. I'm not going to tell you that."

"So you've got to make a phone call?"

"No."

For a moment, he just looked at her. Then he asked, "Are you trying to tell me something, at last?"

Lorna kept her chin defiantly high. "Yes. There were no instructions to get in the first place."

There was another silence, an awful one. Then he asked carefully, "What do you mean?"

Lorna dragged in a painful breath and told the truth. "I made them up. All of them. Since Astrid's phone call at the Boca Grande Café in Winslow last Sunday morning."

Ten

Saying nothing, Adam got out of the car and took her into their room. Lorna sat in a chair at the foot of the bed and told him everything, from the humiliation of Jeffrey's desertion, through her transformation at Astrid's hands, to the misunderstanding about the man she'd kissed in the hallway, and on and on. The deceptions, as she revealed them, seemed never-ending.

Adam sat, unspeaking, in the chair at the small table. Lorna found it impossible to really look at him as deceit upon deceit came to light. She stared instead at a watercolor print over the bed. It was a winter scene of leafless, skeletal trees reaching toward a pewter sky. In the frozen stream beneath the trees, a white-tailed doe attempted to drink.

In its stark way, the picture was lovely, Lorna thought. Not bad at all for a modest motel room in Henryetta, Oklahoma. But though she couldn't stop staring at the picture, she knew that she hated it. The doe looked so cold and lost in its frozen winter world. Like Lorna's own heart, which had basked for a while in the warmth of spring, only to find, too soon, that the winter of cold truth was upon her.

When she was finished, Lorna forced herself to look at Adam.

"That's all of it?" he asked.

Lorna nodded.

The lamp over the table was on, shedding a halo of light on Adam's hair, but shadowing his eyes so it was impossible for her to tell what he was thinking. Lorna realized she was shredding the tissue she held clutched in her hands, so she set it on the low dresser beside her, next to her open suitcase.

"We're meeting my mother tomorrow, then?" he said.

"Yes. Noon. In front of the post office. In Hot Springs—"

"It's okay. I heard you the first time."

"It's true." She looked straight at him, earnestly, and then down at her empty hands. "But I guess I haven't given you much reason to believe anything I say."

"But I do believe you," he said.

"You do?" She knew she should feel relief, but all she could think of was that he'd never forgive her now that he knew how she'd duped him.

He was nodding. "It makes perfect sense when I put it all together."

"Oh," she said in a small voice, vaguely bewildered because he wasn't responding at all the way she'd expected him to. He didn't seem all that angry, for one thing. And he was having no problem accepting the idea that wild Lorna Smith was, in reality, a jilted little mouse who peddled books for a living.

"When you put *what* all together?" she asked, after watching him apprehensively for a moment.

He looked away and cleared his throat. "All right," he said. "You're not the only one with confessing to do. The truth is that I went through your purse in Winslow. And I called a detective I know and had him check you out. When I went to fix the car in Albuquerque, I checked in with him and he told me all about you."

Unbidden, a vivid image flashed through Lorna's mind. She saw herself, writhing on soft cotton sheets in their Albuquerque hotel room, begging Adam to kiss her breasts once more. She had felt then, as all the nights since, like some erotic enchantress.

"You knew?" Her voice came out a weak whisper. Her magical dream of herself as a sensual siren was evaporating in the harsh light of reality. "You knew since Albuquerque who I really was? But you let me go on thinking you just couldn't resist me?"

"Lorna..." His eyes, she could see now, were gentle. Kind. Of course he wasn't angry with her. He felt sorry for her. He probably had felt that way the whole time. "You were enjoying yourself so much. And as soon as I was sure that there was nothing sinister going on with that support group, I didn't see any harm in playing along with your game.''

''Even to the extent of making love with me under false pretenses?'' Lorna could barely get the question out.

''My pretenses,'' he reminded her gently, ''were no more false than yours.''

She had to admit he was right. He, at least, hadn't been pretending to be someone he wasn't. And then there was the fact that she'd so relentlessly thrown herself at him. Once he'd seen through the glitter to the gray mouse beneath, he'd no doubt felt the most graceful way to behave under the circumstances would be to go ahead and indulge her fantasies.

''Lorna, you *did* want to make love with me,'' he said, echoing her own thoughts. ''And when I finally knew who you really were, I didn't see any reason why I had to go on turning you down.''

Lorna stood up. She went to the window and looked out through the miniblinds at the night-lighted pool. ''I see. It was like a kindness,'' she said, her back to him. ''A kindness to a lady who needed to feel desired.''

''It most certainly was not,'' he said. She heard him approaching behind her.

She turned, quickly, and put up a warding-off hand. He stopped in his tracks, showing her his palms.

''Okay,'' he said. ''I won't touch you. But I can't allow you to believe I made love to you for any other reason than that I wanted to. Very much.''

Lorna thought of all the times he had loved her. Of all the crazy things he'd whispered in her ear through all the wonderful nights of their magical week. Surely he was telling the truth now. No man could pretend to be as aroused by a woman as he had seemed to be by her.

But what, on the other hand, did Lorna Smith really know about men and what they were capable of pretending to feel? There hadn't been many in her life, and she'd always said she didn't understand them one bit.

Witness Jeffrey. She'd been so sure he was the ideal man for her. And he'd seemed to feel the same way—right up until he'd dumped her. And if she couldn't hold a rather shy, unassuming accountant, what had possessed her to imagine she could keep a man like Adam Gantry?

Adam was so handsome. So intelligent. So perfect. So totally beyond what a woman like herself could ever dream of holding. The fantasy Lorna might have wanted him and enchanted him and claimed him for her own. But the fantasy was over; reality had to be faced.

There was absolutely no point, Lorna decided then, in pursuing this subject any further. She'd deceived him; he'd misled her. Their time together would end tomorrow at noon, and that was all there was to it.

"I'm tired, Adam," she said. "And we should start early in the morning."

He looked at her sympathetically. "I understand. We can hash out the rest of this later, after we've met up with Astrid and wrapped up that whole mess."

"There really isn't much more to say," Lorna told him.

"We'll talk about it later," he insisted quietly. "I realize I invaded your privacy in going through your belongings. And I apologize."

"We were both in the wrong," she said quickly. "Let's just let it go, okay?"

"All right, for now."

There ensued another of those awful silences where he kept looking at her so understandingly that she wanted to scream.

At last she said hesitantly, "I guess I'll go brush my teeth, then."

"Good idea," he replied, and she thought he sounded relieved that this embarrassing conversation was coming to an end. "We should try to get some sleep." But then he just stood there, blocking her way to the other room, looking at her as if he was waiting for her to say something more.

"Excuse me," she murmured.

"Oh, sorry," he said, like a stranger who had accidentally blocked her way on a public street.

He stepped aside. She edged around him and made a beeline for the bathroom door.

Once in there, Lorna brushed her teeth and cleaned her face as fast as she could. It was so unpleasant, after all, having to look at her own lackluster reflection in the mirror. She kept thinking, miserably, that it was all just like the old fairy tale. Midnight had come, and Cinderella was a dreary little nothing once again.

When she emerged from the bathroom, Adam took his turn. Lorna climbed into one of the two double beds. She turned over and buried her head in the blankets when she heard him come back out, praying he'd just climb into the other bed and not decide that anything at all needed to be said about the sudden change in their sleeping arrangements.

But he didn't make it easy on her. She heard the brushing of his bare feet on the carpet as he came to the side of her bed.

"I take it you're trying to tell me something, wrapped in those blankets as if they were armor." His voice was flat.

She tried to go on pretending she was asleep, but it was no use. It was emotional agony, lying there while he stood behind her and waited for her to get up the nerve to reply to his question.

She pushed the covers away from her face and turned her head to look at him. "I'm really tired."

"Are you saying you prefer to sleep alone?"

"Yes." How a single syllable could crack in the middle, she didn't know, but it did.

For a moment she thought he would argue with her and a tiny flame of hope flared in her heart. But then he shrugged, and the weak flame went out.

"All right," he said in that same bland voice. Then he turned away and she heard him pulling down the covers on the other bed.

The next morning they were on the road by seven. The five-hour drive to Hot Springs seemed never-ending. Confined in a limited space yet with an emotional chasm yawning between them, both Lorna and Adam tacitly retreated behind a painful mutual courtesy.

The green and rolling farmlands of Oklahoma slowly turned to dense Arkansas woods. Lorna commented on the beauty of the hillsides of ferny sumac. Adam agreed; the scenery was lovely.

They left the main highway at Russellville, taking a two-lane road that wove in and out of close-growing trees until they reached Hot Springs, a resort city which wrapped itself around the national park of the same name. The highway they traveled became Park Avenue and then they were passing the famous Tussaud Wax Museum, Park Avenue having flowed into Central.

They came then to Bathhouse Row, where for more than a century travelers had come to take the healing waters of the mineral springs that welled up from deep underground.

"Astrid says my grandmother worked as a masseuse at the Fordyce," Adam said, as they passed a bathhouse of that name.

"Really?" Lorna responded, too brightly. "How interesting."

In no time at all they reached Reserve Avenue. Adam turned left and there was the imposing brick post office. Lorna spotted Astrid immediately. She was standing by Lorna's shining Mercedes, wearing a jewel-green cotton dress, her blond hair gleaming in the noonday sun.

She'd seen Adam's car and was waving blithely with her free hand. Her other hand was twined most companionably with the hand of the tall, distinguished-looking man at her side.

"Is that who I hope it is?" Lorna asked.

"Yes," Adam said. "Maxwell Hollander." He smiled, looking rather abashed. "It appears they managed to work it out between themselves without my help." He cast Lorna a wry glance. "Just as you said they would."

Lorna looked back at him, sure all her love and longing were written plain as day on her scrubbed-clean face. Then she remembered how she must look to him, now she'd finally been honest and admitted who she truly was. She'd scraped her hair back and anchored it with a rubber band, and she hadn't even allowed herself the luxury of lipstick.

"Lorna," he said softly.

She knew he was about to start being kind again. She tore her gaze from his beloved face and pointed out the window.

"There's a parking space. Right there," she said.

As soon as he stopped the car, Lorna jumped out of it. Astrid ran toward her, laughing, pulling Maxwell Hollander along behind. When Lorna and Astrid were face-to-face at last, Astrid froze for a moment, like a beautiful, exotic bird hovering in midair. Her bright emerald glance darted from her son to Lorna and then back again.

"Well," she said, her soft Arkansas drawl more pronounced than ever. "We're all here at last." She turned to Maxwell and smiled, a smile of love and belonging. "Together," she said. "Just as we were meant to be."

Maxwell Hollander looked down at her like he'd like to hustle her off somewhere and prove to her just exactly how together they were. Astrid's smile widened.

Then Astrid was looking at Lorna again, and holding out her arms. Lorna went into them, hugging Astrid and breathing in the exotic, haunting scent of her friend's perfume.

"What's this," the husky voice whispered in her ear. "A little sackcloth and ashes?"

Lorna blinked and pulled back. "Excuse me?" she said, pretending she didn't know what Astrid meant. But of course, she did. She thought huffily, How dare she insinuate that I'm punishing myself?

"Never mind." Astrid's voice was mild. She pressed the keys to the Mercedes into Lorna's palm. Then she turned to her son and hugged him as she had Lorna. "Baby, you look terrific," she said when she let him go. "All rested and tan."

"Thank you, Mother," Adam said good-naturedly.

"I think it's time we had a short family conference." Astrid took Adam's arm. "We'll just take a little walk. Maxwell, keep Lorna company?"

Maxwell gave Lorna a friendly wink. "I'll do my best."

Astrid and Adam strolled off together toward Central Avenue. Lorna tried her best to make polite conversation with Astrid's fiancé as she waited for the other two to return. But in the corner of her eye, she kept seeing her car and thinking of one word: escape.

She needed to get away, off to herself. But she knew she couldn't do it without telling Adam she was going. It was only fair, after all they'd shared, no matter how illusory, that she tell him goodbye at the end. Otherwise, she'd be running away. And Lorna Smith was a straightforward sort of person who never cut and ran.

But that's exactly what you'll be doing, a voice suspiciously like her nagging conscience whispered in her ear, *if you leave without telling him how you really feel for him. If you run out of his life without saying that you love him.*

Say she loved him, out loud? Lorna cringed at the thought. Hadn't she already made a big enough fool of herself, pretending to be someone she wasn't and never would be? It would only serve to compound their mutual embarrassment if she threw herself at him again, this time with protestations of undying love.

"Are you all right?" Maxwell Hollander was asking. "You look a little pale."

Lorna forced a smile. "We got an early start this morning," she excused lamely. "And I didn't get much sleep."

Astrid and Adam came strolling back. "That was quick," Maxwell said.

Adam put on a chastened expression. "There wasn't much to say except, 'I'm sorry, Mother, and I promise to let you run your own life from here on out.'"

"A mother could do worse than to have a son who cares so much," Maxwell pointed out.

"That's what I said," Astrid beamed. "Now what about lunch? There's a great little restaurant called Dad's Place over at the hotel we're staying in."

Lorna could bear it no longer. She *had* to get away. She spoke quickly, without stopping to think how very gauche she was going to sound. "I, um, really need to be on my way."

There was a deadly silence.

Adam said, "What?"

"Back to L.A." Lorna's voice sounded ridiculously weak to her own ears. "It's a long drive."

Adam was looking at her through eyes like green ice. "You're leaving? Just like that?"

Astrid said tactfully, "We'll just leave you two alone for a few minutes."

"No," Adam said. "If Lorna wants to go I would never try to stop her. I've learned my lesson about interfering in other people's lives."

*   *   *   *   *

Eleven

Once behind the wheel of her car, Lorna drove with single-minded determination. She did her best to keep her mind a blank, concentrating only on the road before her and on what she could see in her side and rearview mirrors. She tried to completely disengage her emotions, to imagine herself as a machine that knew one thing only: how to drive a car. Cutting off her emotions was imperative, because she knew that as soon as she let herself start to feel again, what she'd be feeling would be pain.

But in spite of all her efforts, she couldn't completely keep the unwelcome images at bay. They rose up tauntingly between herself and the black ribbon of the highway. She'd see again the rocklike set to Adam's jaw as he'd tossed her suitcases into the trunk of her car and slammed the lid. She'd hear his voice.

"That should do it. You've got everything that's yours."

All except my heart, she'd think, and her throat would close up dangerously. Then she'd swallow and blink and force her traitorous mind back to the job at hand: driving the car.

The Arkansas hills melted into Oklahoma farmlands and then the stands of wheat and corn became the rolling, rich grasslands of the Texas panhandle. Lorna hardly noticed the changing of the land as she raced back the way they had come.

She drove until midnight. Then she realized that her eyes were burning and her hands were stiff from clutching the steering wheel. To push herself farther would have been to endanger herself and other travelers.

Amarillo lay before her, and she stopped there, checking into the first motel she found. She went straight to bed.

And she realized after an hour of punching her pillow and staring at a faint watermark on the ceiling that bed was the worst place in the world for her to be. Somehow, in the space of a week, she'd become like a woman married for fifty years, who'd never slept a night away from her husband.

She couldn't relax without Adam beside her. She missed his warmth against her back, his breath in her hair. She decided, with the first stirring of humor since the truth had been revealed, that Adam Gantry had stolen her heart and in return left her with a bad case of insomnia.

Just before dawn tinted the sky, Lorna gave up on chasing sleep. She rose and took to the road once again. But she didn't get far. Just west of the city, as the sun rose behind her, she came to the ten nose-down Cadillacs in the middle of the field.

And suddenly, all unbidden, she was seeing herself and Adam racing across the ploughed, dark earth. She could hear her own carefree laughter as she towed the balking Adam along behind, until they stood at the foot of the half-buried cars.

She felt again his arms going round her, and his lips on hers, stealing her breath.

Why Adam, she'd asked him, *what's happened to you?*

Something wonderful, he'd told her, *something absolutely wild....*

Now, alone behind the wheel of her car, Lorna's eyes were brimming. There was no way to stop it. She could barely see the road. Giving in at last to all the emotions she'd been fleeing, Lorna pulled over to the shoulder and burst into tears.

She sat there, sobbing, until a highway patrol car pulled in behind her.

She dried her eyes and blew her nose as a patrolwoman got out of the car and came around to Lorna's side window. At the officer's discreet tap, Lorna rolled the window down.

"Driver's license and registration, please," said the patrolwoman.

Lorna silently handed them over. The woman studied them and passed them back. Then she took off her military-style dark glasses to reveal eyes as blue as Texas skies. "Is there a problem here?"

"Just a minor breakdown, Officer," Lorna managed to say ruefully.

For a moment, the blue eyes studied Lorna keenly. Then she said, "Will you be all right, then?"

"I'll be fine." Lorna forced a tremulous smile.

"You'll have to pull out. No stopping on the shoulder except for emergencies."

"I'll pull out right after you," Lorna said, her gaze wandering once again to the row of half-buried luxury cars.

"Procedure is that you pull out first," the officer instructed.

"Oh. Okay."

The woman intercepted Lorna's glance and laughed. "They're something, aren't they? I drive past them maybe ten times a day sometimes, and they still make me smile."

"Only in America," Lorna said, thinking with a tender pang of Adam.

"Texas, to be specific," drawled the patrolwoman. "Now get that fancy foreign car out on the road where it belongs."

Lorna did as instructed and once she was safely rolling toward Los Angeles again, it occurred to her that the car was too quiet. She turned on the radio and punched buttons until she found a country and western station. She sang along, switching stations when the signal got weak, all the way to Albuquerque, which she reached in the early afternoon.

She pulled into a gas station just east of the city to fuel up and visit the rest room.

"Yuck," she said trenchantly to her bedraggled reflection in the metal mirror over the basin. It was then that she decided to stop in Albuquerque for the night.

And, of course, she knew just the hotel to stay in. And just the suite she wanted.

"That's a two-bedroom suite," the desk clerk reminded her.

"I know," Lorna replied. "But it's my favorite." She granted him a mischievous grin.

"Well, then," he said. "As the lady desires."

"My sentiments exactly," Lorna remarked, reaching for the key.

She went to the pool first, for an invigorating swim. And then she made use of the sauna and steam room. She had a massage, luxuriating in every moment of pounding and pummeling at the hands of an expert.

Then she showered, and fixed her hair and makeup. Finally she donned a fuchsia-pink bustier sundress and matching bolero jacket.

A final twirl before the dressing room mirror told her just what she'd begun to perceive outside of Amarillo. The beautiful woman who smiled naughtily at her in the mirror was as much herself as the serious gray mouse who'd studied library science in college and owned The Book Nook.

There's a siren inside every one of us, Astrid had said. *It's just a matter of bringing her out.*

"And, once she's out, believing she's real," Lorna added to the mirror.

It had never been, as Lorna had assumed, a question of believing in Astrid. The challenge had always been to believe in herself and in all she could be.

Such insights made Lorna realize she was starving. She considered room service and then decided she would enjoy the sounds of other diners talking and laughing around her.

She descended to the restaurant and ordered a cocktail before deciding on what to eat. The drink was something called a Triple Enchantment. Frothy and yellow, it had two paper sombreros on toothpicks sticking out of it, not to mention a pink swizzle stick bearing chunks of maraschino cherries and pineapple.

Lorna savored the foot-high drink slowly, winking once at the man at the next table who promptly dropped his fork. She was considering the wisdom of ordering a second drink when she saw the tall, blond-haired man striding in her direction.

Lorna slurped up the last of her drink, hoping the alcohol content would slow down her heart, which suddenly seemed to be doing calisthenics beneath her bustier dress. And as Adam stalked so resolutely toward her, she decided that a very nice day in Albuquerque had just become perfect.

Because he looked wonderful. His tie was slightly askew and his shirt just a little wrinkled. His eyes were a little red. Of course, he hadn't slept for two nights. But he looked better than a Fudgie Bar, and more intoxicating than a Triple Enchantment.

"My mother called me a damn fool," he said when he reached her side. His gaze devoured her, and Lorna felt her skin tingling. She was remembering how very pleasurable it was to be devoured by Adam Gantry.

"Astrid is so succinct," Lorna said, then added, "I imagine she had a few things to say about me, as well."

Adam snorted. "One or two. But I'll let her tell you herself when you meet in your support group back in L.A."

Lorna took a miniature sombrero from her drink and twirled it between her fingers. "How did you know where to find me?"

"I didn't. It was purely a hunch. The same way Maxwell found my mother."

Lorna stopped twirling the sombrero. "You mean he went to Hot Springs on a hunch?"

Adam nodded. "He knew she was born there, and that she still owns her mother's house out by Lake Ouachita. That's where he found her."

"In her mother's house?"

"Yes."

"How beautiful," Lorna said, twirling her sombrero again and pondering the mysteries of love. Then she asked, "And you're telling me that you had a hunch I'd be here?"

"Yes." Adam looked around and realized that the waiter was hovering nearby, waiting discreetly to learn whether Adam intended to eat or move on. "Let's go to your room."

Lorna considered this suggestion. "If I go with you—"

"It's not a question of if."

"I thought you said you were through interfering in other people's lives."

"I am. Except for your life. I'm going to keep on interfering in your life until—"

"Yes?"

"Until we get it right. If you go with me, what?"

Over the twirling sombrero, she memorized his handsome face. "Never mind. I forgot." And she had, too. Because all she could think of was that Adam was here, again, in Albuquerque with her and that all was at last right with the world.

For endless moments, they stared at each other. Then the waiter said in a thoroughly incongruous east coast accent, "Go with him, already. You can eat anytime."

In spite of the fact that he'd served her no more than one Triple Enchantment, Lorna left that waiter a generous tip.

Outside beyond the balcony, the sun still hovered, hot and orange, above the Rio Grande. The glass door had been left slightly ajar, so the filmy curtains moved in the early-evening breeze.

"We need to talk," Adam said.

"Yes, Adam." Lorna slowly peeled off her bolero jacket and then tossed it onto a side chair.

For a moment, Adam seemed to forget what he was saying as he stared at the gleaming skin of Lorna's shoulders. Then he recollected himself. "There are a thousand things that need to be settled between us. There'll be no more running away from this thing until we've hashed it all out."

"You are so right," Lorna replied, easing off her high-heeled shoes.

"The problem was that I didn't expect you to take my knowing who you really were so hard," Adam said. "In hindsight, of course, I can see just what happened. Since you were insecure after what happened with your ex-fiancé, you assumed that no man would really want you if he knew your real self."

"That's true," Lorna said.

"But you had it all wrong," Adam told her. "I wanted you even more, when I learned about the other aspects of you."

"You did?"

"Yes. The woman I knew first was enchanting and beautiful and exciting to be around. But it's the part of you that you call mousy who gives you depth and gentleness and those haunting secrets behind your eyes. I made love with you because, once I knew all of you, there was no way I could have stopped myself."

"You mean I completely broke down your famous self-control?"

He nodded, looking grim. "Broke it down and stomped on it and hung it out to dry. And then, when you confessed everything in Oklahoma, I realized I was going to have to come clean, too. And the minute I did, I could see the mistake I had made by not telling you sooner. You cut yourself off from me completely. I told myself you needed some time to digest everything. Then in Hot Springs, out of the blue, you announced you were leaving. I couldn't decide whether to strangle you or beg you to stay, so I let you go."

"Poor Adam," she said softly.

"Poor Adam?" he repeated. "Is that all you have to say?"

In answer, she padded over to him on nylon-clad feet and offered him her back, gently sweeping aside the veil of her hair. It was extremely gratifying to hear his sharp intake of breath.

"Would you help me with this zipper?" she asked.

The question hung in the air for a moment. Then the zipper skittered down. She felt the evening breeze on the small of her back and it was her turn to gasp as his index finger skimmed her exposed flesh, starting at her nape and caressing down the length of her spine. "We're getting off the subject," he murmured huskily.

"I disagree," she purred. "I think we're really starting to communicate now."

His finger trailed back up to toy with the short wisps of hair on her neck. "You do, do you?"

"Absolutely. Kiss me there, Adam," she said. And felt the velvety touch of his lips at her nape and then traveling deliciously downward and back up again.

"I love when you do that," she said.

He grasped her waist and pulled her back against him. He breathed into her ear, "You *are* bad."

"Umm." She took his hands and helped them to peel the dress to her waist. And then she laid his palms against the swelling curves beneath her lacy strapless bra. "But only with you."

"Exactly," he said, his voice rough and low, a sound that stroked each of her nerve endings in turn. "That's what drives me crazy."

She slithered around and danced out away from him, laughing with pleasure. Then she unhooked the bit of lace and let the bra fall to the floor.

"You mean like out of control?" she asked.

"I mean like absolutely wild," he said, as he came to her. His hands found her, pushing the dress off her hips and making short work of her panty hose, as well.

And as soon as he had her completely revealed to his sight, she began tugging at his tie. Slowly, sensuously, she snaked it from around his neck and tossed it across the room. Then she unbuttoned his slightly wrinkled shirt, and pushed it off his shoulders. And after that, lingering long about it, she gathered the soft cotton of his undershirt up from beneath his belt, guided it over his muscled rib cage and smoothly pulled it off over his head.

"You're so beautiful, Adam," she said with a sigh as she stepped back to admire the sculpted perfection of his torso and arms. "I guess there's something to be said for discipline, after all."

His appreciative gaze licked over her, showing her her own beauty more clearly than words ever could. "Come back here," he said.

She sighed, opening her arms to him as he brought her close, chest to breast. When his mouth closed over hers, she opened herself without hesitation to the questing entry of his tongue, meeting it with her own, and reveling in the pure eroticism of his tongue stroking hers, and hers stroking back.

The passionate kiss went on and on, as she unbuckled his cordovan belt and slid it through its loops, unhooked his slacks and unzipped his zipper.

In no time at all, they stood nude before each other in the shadowed early evening light.

"No more secrets, Lorna?" he breathed, as he looked at all of her again, from wild, curling hair to slim, fuchsia-tipped toes.

She faced him proudly, glorious in her nakedness and set free by the desire she could see in his eyes. "None, Adam. You know everything now."

He brought her close once more. She moaned as they slid to the thick, soft carpet at the foot of the bed.

He kissed her everywhere. And she, being wild and unashamed, kissed him everywhere right back. Until there was nothing in the darkening room but soft cries of pleasure and husky encouragements, the thrill of an intimate touch and the answering gasp of delight.

Lorna rose up above him, at last, as she loved to do, and poised herself to take him within her. But he stopped her, and he held her with his jade-green gaze and his strong hands at her waist.

"Say it first," he said, his voice deep with his need of her.

She wanted him; her body strained blindly toward his. But still his arms held her slightly away. "Say it, Lorna. Tell me. Now. As you take me inside you. We'll say it together, what we should have said then."

She smiled, with the pleasure and the wonder of it. Slowly, she claimed him and as she did, she said, "I love you, Adam."

And he said, "I love you, Lorna."

And they said it together as their bodies met and mated. Over and over, as true lovers have always done.

In mutual surrender to something bigger and grander than either ever is alone.

And then words became impossible as once more they found their freedom, locked tight in the tender bondage of each other's arms.

"Marry me?" he asked simply, when they could both talk again.

"Um, yes, I think I'll do that." She sighed, toying with the crisp hairs on his broad chest.

"You only think?" He lifted his head from the carpet and attempted to glare at her.

She slid up his chest and kissed his chin. "Absolutely, my darling. I'll marry you. Yes."

"That's better." He relaxed again.

She rested her tousled head on his chest and listened with drowsy pleasure to the sound of his heart. "I suppose with Maxwell in Arkansas, you're going to need to go back to that exemplary law firm of yours right away."

"For at least a week or two," he told her. "But then Max has promised to return and I could manage some more time."

Lazily, he reached for the pale yellow comforter on the bed and settled it over the two of them. A pillow conveniently dropped to the carpet with the blanket, and Lorna arranged it under his head.

"How about Palm Springs?" he asked, when they were cozy and warm in their nest on the floor. "You could end up having your honeymoon there, after all."

She shook her head. "We've been there."

"Well, then?"

"I'd like to see the Great Lakes. And meet an Eskimo. And wrestle an alligator in the Florida Keys. And then there's Europe, and China and Australia and—"

"Whoa," he said, laughing. "One country at a time."

"You're right." She planted a light, dewy kiss on his neck. "And it doesn't really matter where we go anyway. As long as we're together." She nibbled on the place she'd kissed, and felt him stirring again beneath the yellow blanket.

"Why, Adam," she murmured, "what's happening to you?"

"Something wonderful," he told her. "Something absolutely wild."

* * * * *

HARLEQUIN®

Don't miss these Harlequin favorites by some of our most
distinguished authors!
And now, you can receive a discount by ordering two or more titles!

HT #25663	THE LAWMAN by Vicki Lewis Thompson	$3.25 U.S. ☐/$3.75 CAN.	☐
HP #11788	THE SISTER SWAP by Susan Napier	$3.25 U.S. ☐/$3.75 CAN.	☐
HR #03293	THE MAN WHO CAME FOR CHRISTMAS by Bethany Campbell	$2.99 U.S. ☐/$3.50 CAN.	☐
HS #70667	FATHERS & OTHER STRANGERS by Evelyn Crowe	$3.75 U.S. ☐/$4.25 CAN.	☐
HI #22198	MURDER BY THE BOOK by Margaret St. George	$2.89	☐
HAR #16520	THE ADVENTURESS by M.J. Rodgers	$3.50 U.S. ☐/$3.99 CAN.	☐
HH #28885	DESERT ROGUE by Erin Yorke	$4.50 U.S. ☐/$4.99 CAN.	☐

(limited quantities available on certain titles)

	AMOUNT	$
DEDUCT:	**10% DISCOUNT FOR 2+ BOOKS**	$
ADD:	**POSTAGE & HANDLING**	$
	($1.00 for one book, 50¢ for each additional)	
	APPLICABLE TAXES**	$_____
	TOTAL PAYABLE	$_____
	(check or money order—please do not send cash)	

To order, complete this form and send it, along with a check or money order for the
total above, payable to Harlequin Books, to: **In the U.S.:** 3010 Walden Avenue,
P.O. Box 9047, Buffalo, NY 14269-9047; **In Canada:** P.O. Box 613, Fort Erie, Ontario,
L2A 5X3.

Name:_____

Address:_____ City:_____

State/Prov.:_____ Zip/Postal Code:_____

**New York residents remit applicable sales taxes.
Canadian residents remit applicable GST and provincial taxes. HBACK-JS3

Look us up on-line at: http://www.romance.net

Harlequin Romance ®

Delightful

Affectionate

Romantic

Emotional

Tender

Original

Daring

Riveting

Enchanting

Adventurous

Moving

Harlequin Romance—the
series that has it all!

HROM-G

HARLEQUIN  PRESENTS®

HARLEQUIN PRESENTS
men you won't be able to resist falling in love with...

HARLEQUIN PRESENTS
women who have feelings just like your own...

HARLEQUIN PRESENTS
powerful passion in exotic international settings...

HARLEQUIN PRESENTS
intense, dramatic stories that will keep you turning
to the very last page...

HARLEQUIN PRESENTS
The world's bestselling romance series!

Harlequin® Historical

If you're a serious fan of historical romance,
then you're in luck!

Harlequin Historicals brings you
stories by bestselling authors, rising new stars
and talented first-timers.

Ruth Langan & Theresa Michaels
Mary McBride & Cheryl St. John
Margaret Moore & Merline Lovelace
Julie Tetel & Nina Beaumont
Susan Amarillas & Ana Seymour
Deborah Simmons & Linda Castle
Cassandra Austin & Emily French
Miranda Jarrett & Suzanne Barclay
DeLoras Scott & Laurie Grant...

You'll never run out of favorites.

Harlequin Historicals...they're too good to miss!

HH-GEN

HARLEQUIN®

A M E R I C A N ❖ R O M A N C E®

LOOK FOR OUR FOUR FABULOUS MEN!

Each month some of today's bestselling authors bring
four new fabulous men to Harlequin American Romance.
Whether they're rebel ranchers, millionaire power brokers
or sexy single dads, they're all gallant princes—and
they're all ready to sweep you into lighthearted fantasies
and contemporary fairy tales where anything is possible
and where all your dreams come true!

You don't even have to make a wish...Harlequin American
Romance will grant your every desire!

Look for Harlequin American Romance wherever Harlequin
books are sold!

WAYS TO *UNEXPECTEDLY* MEET MR. RIGHT:

♡ Go out with the sexy-sounding stranger your daughter secretly set you up with through a personal ad.

♡ RSVP yes to a wedding invitation—soon it might be your turn to say "I do!"

♡ Receive a marriage proposal by mail—from a man you've never met....

These are just a few of the unexpected ways that written communication leads to love in Silhouette Yours Truly.

Each month, look for two fast-paced, fun and flirtatious Yours Truly novels (with entertaining treats and sneak previews in the back pages) by some of your favorite authors—and some who are sure to become favorites.

YOURS TRULY™:
Love—when you least expect it!

Tom Selleck
and
Jillie Mack

The first time Tom Selleck of "Magnum P.I." fame saw Jillie Mack, a London stage actor, he was smitten. So much so, in fact, that he was too shy to ask her out! Luckily, a mutual friend convinced Tom to call Jillie, and the two hit it off smashingly.

After their first date, Jillie was quoted as saying, "He is very polite and gentlemanly. He is the most complete man I have ever met. Even more marvelous than he looks and sounds. He is everything I have ever looked for in a man."

They were married in Lake Tahoe in August of 1987.

B-TOM